RUNNING

B.B. TAYLOR

TINY TREE

Running
Published in 2024 by
Tiny Tree Books
West Wing Studios
Unit 166, The Mall
Luton, LU1 2TL
tinytreebooks.com

Text copyright © B.B. Taylor

The right of B.B. Taylor to be identified as the author of this work has been asserted in accordance with the Copyright, Designs and Patents Act 1988.

All rights reserved. No reproduction, copy or transmission of this publication may be made without express prior written permission. No paragraph of this publication may be reproduced, copied or transmitted except with express prior written permission or in accordance with the provisions of the Copyright Act 1956 (as amended). Any person who commits any unauthorised act in relation to this publication may be liable to criminal prosecution and civil claims for damage.

All characters appearing in this work are fictitious.
Any resemblance to real persons, living
or dead, is purely coincidental.

Trigger Warning
This book contains content that may make
some readers uncomfortable, including
scenes involving violence and blood.

Acknowledgements

There are always so many people to acknowledge when you're a writer and always the risk of missing someone off or leaving someone out, so many people have been important in my writing journey and continue to give me the drive to continue no matter how hard the road ahead can seem. So, I thank a few here and ask all those not mentioned to remember how important you all are and how I wouldn't still be writing without you.

Through all of it though has been my husband who believes in me even when I don't believe in myself, I thank you for being my best friend and my rock and my daughter Bailey who embraces my need to write and is always happy to keep me topped up on sugary tea. Mr Bob Stone who patiently reads my million ideas and helps me bounce my ideas onto the page, even when he's got his own amazing books to write and who has championed my books for over a decade in his beautiful shop The Write Blend.

To my writing family who cheer each other on, especially my SCBWI family and particularly Sarah Broadley who first saw a glimpse of this book nearly ten years ago at critique and always seems to know the perfect time to check in. A massive thank you to Kathryn Evans, Teri Terry, Sue Wallman and all the other authors who I look up to, who have kindly read the book as I nervously entered into their world of Young Adult writing.

A huge thank you to James and Ant at Tiny Tree who I'm so excited to be working with again, who put so much love into children's and young adult books bringing something special to the book world.

But most importantly thank you to the readers who have been on this journey with me for over a decade. It's time we take that next leap together and I hope I do you proud. Without you, there is no me.

B.B. Taylor

For anyone who was told they weren't good enough, keep running after your dreams.

One: Mairi

Hovering over the lifeless body before me, hollow and numb, my hands trembled; betraying me as I tried to keep control. It didn't last long before autopilot took over. Emotions would catch up later; they always did – like the dam breaking – but for now I needed to concentrate. The blood, that had only moments ago flowed so freely from his neck, now pooled around his lifeless corpse, soaking into his expensive looking suit like some garish Halloween costume. The spattered drops on my lips left the aftertaste of copper on the tip of my tongue and my mind momentarily drifted.

I'd been running for as long as I could remember. Running not only for my freedom but for my very life. Nameless faces kept coming and their target was clear. Me. Mairi.

I didn't want to hurt anyone. The scars it left on my heart were unbearable, but it was either them or me. Survival had been hard-wired in. I wasn't ready to die; not sure if I ever would be, but I wasn't going to go quietly.

Have you ever looked death in the eye? I have, and I've seen the Grim Reaper staring straight back at me too many times. A cat may have nine lives but I've used all mine and borrowed some as well.

Blood; it's such a strange thing. Seen as a life force and seen as death, yet there is a strange beauty to it. Like the silky petals of a red rose surrounded by the spike of its thorns.

It was everywhere around me. So much blood I might as well have been swimming in it. I doubt if all the oceans in the world could ever wash it away, unable to tell what was mine and what wasn't anymore. But I knew they would be coming. I couldn't stay still for too long. They wanted what I had and I wouldn't live long if they got it.

Checking the body, I looked for any cash. Cards were useless, too easy to trace, but cash, now that was something I could use. Once I was sure I had gotten everything, I covered myself with my previously discarded coat; attempting to hide the bloody artwork decorating my clothing. Grabbing my small bag, I made a hasty exit, keeping to the shadows and avoiding any unnecessary attention.

A short distance away there was a run-down bed and breakfast. I didn't want any contact with people but I needed to lay low for a while, to breathe, maybe puke, or both. Thankfully, the young guy on the desk didn't ask any questions and took my cash promptly with hardly a glance in my direction, more interested in the music blaring from his headphones than small talk.

Entering the battered room, the mouldy smell assaulted my nostrils. Damp splodges evident on every wall. Locking the doors and checking all the windows were secure, I closed all the curtains. My ritual for entering any building: ensuring I wasn't followed, securing the perimeter and staying for as short a period as possible. I couldn't work out how they were tracking me but they were good. I had no phone, no technology to trace, not even a watch. Yet I barely managed to keep half a step ahead of them, never able to look forward without first looking back.

Dropping my pitiful excuse for a bag on the bed I headed towards the bathroom. Removing the knife from my boot, I stripped off the blood-soaked clothes and turned on the shower. Surprisingly, it provided me with hot water; the steam filling the cold bathroom air like dragon's breath. It had been a while since I'd been able to feel physically clean – as for emotionally clean, I wasn't sure I'd ever know that feeling again.

Dumping the clothes into the sink I had filled with hot water, I stepped towards the shower, grabbing the knife and taking it in too. Even naked it was never wise to leave yourself exposed. I placed the blade, which had become an unwanted extension of myself, on the shower shelf at eye line while pulling my aching body under the scalding water. I let it trickle down, hissing through gritted teeth as it burnt against my blood-soaked skin. It reminded me I was still alive, still surviving… for now, but I was getting tired and losing the will to keep fighting.

As the blood trickled down my pale skin, I felt fresher and cleaner and it was now more apparent from where my own blood had originated. A nice clean slash across my thigh and another to match down my arm. Once I was as clean as I was going to get I turned the water off and exited the shower, blade once again in my grip.

Searching my small, tattered bag, I found the old box I was looking for. Barely anything in it except the remnants of a sewing kit, but beggars couldn't be choosers. The two wounds were as clean as they were going to get, so I ran the old sewing needle under the piping-hot tap for a few seconds. My trembling fingers threaded the needle with the cleanest thread I could find, putting my blade handle in my mouth and biting down as I began to sew. I hated sewing and my lines were always uneven, but it had its practicalities.

Trying not to think of the searing pain slicing through my body, I concentrated on making the stitches as tight as possible; not wanting any gaps where the wounds could split later. The sharp stabbing of the needle wasn't as bad as the grating tug of the coarse thread being pulled through my skin, rubbing against the exposed flesh, stitch after stitch, dragging the wound tighter, not allowing my body to slip into shock before I had finished my task. Biting harder against the hard wood, I fought against the tears, my face scrunching as my insides turned.

I finished tying off the end and used the blade to cut the excess. I heaved as my stomach betrayed me and I tried not to empty its contents.

There was a noise outside and I froze as I saw shadows against the windows. I could make out two broad figures, highlighted by the outside lights. I stood and pressed my back against the door, keeping an eye on the window and removing the towel altogether.

I listened, not daring to breathe and I could hear two men talking to the guy from the front desk; the one who had seen me check in and had taken my money. I stayed still, hoping it was a case of my paranoia overworking.

"Have you seen a young girl? Late teens? Possibly looking quite confused and distressed?" The voice had a clinically authoritarian tone.

"Nah mate, only female checked in is Dotty, one of our regulars. Completely batty though if you want to take her instead," the clerk replied chuckling.

"There was someone hanging around outside earlier though, looking like they were deciding whether to come in, but they went off down towards the motorway junction. Could have been a girl." I breathed a temporary sigh of relief; I wasn't out of the woods yet though.

"Well, if she does come back you need to ring us immediately. She is a very unwell individual and we are… erm… concerned for her safety."

I bit my tongue. There was only one thing they were concerned about.

"Yeah, no problem dudes! Is there a reward with that?" Looked like he'd changed his mind.

"Yes," the closest replied. "Her safety is of the utmost importance to her family." My foot started twitching and my chest began to tighten. Trying to steady my breathing, I waited for the betrayal but it didn't come. Instead they left, racing in the direction he had given. That wouldn't distract them for long.

Two: Alistair

His steps echoed down the polished corridor. Stopping momentarily, he adjusted his tie before continuing; there was no avoiding it. His brain contemplating all the possible outcomes, he reached the intended door and stopped to adjust his clothes again. Image was everything; a shield and weapon, a lesson he'd learnt well. Taking a deep breath and clearing his head, he took the plunge. It had been a very long time since he had been summoned and it was never a comfortable experience.

He could still vividly recall the first time he had been called, when he was much younger and more naive to the world. He had arrived, eager, desperate to impress and even more so to make his mark on the world. He wanted his name to live forever, his work was ground-breaking.

But at what cost?

They had promised him the world: Money, the best facilities and equipment and of course, creative free reign. Something the government had never done; with their tight budgets and mountains of red tape, they had stifled him at every turn and left him frustrated and confined by their rules and regulations. Then, a light at the end of the tunnel. The hand of opportunity extended without any questions asked. He should have known there would be a cost.

Oh well, the deal had been done. No time for ifs and buts, they were waiting and that was never a good thing. Entering the room silently, he took his place at the top of the conference room. The dimly lit room only revealed the shadowed outlines of those sat and presumably staring at him.

It had been rumoured that the Shadow Board had always existed, but never proven. They were above reproach, outside the judgement of the everyday world, and he had given them their greatest toy.

Clearing his voice, squinting from the bright light focussed solely on him as he stood centre stage, he spoke softly. "You wished to see me?"

"Professor Crowland, how nice of you to join us. We have had some disturbing news brought to our attention, would you like to shed any light on this?"

Just as he was about to try and explain the voice spoke again, "Professor we haven't got all day."

They weren't particularly known for their humour or their patience, so there was no point trying to soften the blow. "Well, yes I didn't wish to disturb you with the matter. I've got it under control, so there seemed to be no point bothering you over something that will be shortly rectified."

He waited, knowing the answer wouldn't satisfy but hoping he sounded more assured than he actually was.

"Well, we think this is slightly more of a concern than you seem to give it credit for; you have lost one and if it gets into the wrong hands, we could all be exposed."

A gulp escaped. The GAP taskforce had been set up many years ago with one purpose: to find him and the institute. They had discovered his side-line of work and hadn't been too pleased, so he had swiftly relocated off the grid. He knew he couldn't let them interfere with his work; he had come too far and sacrificed too much already; this was just too important. He cleared his throat, then spoke again.

"It was merely a mix-up with security who have been dealt with already, I already have a team recovering the missing product. The GAP task force is completely unaware it even exists and I have someone on the inside reporting back weekly. I assure you the programme is secure."

The silence was painfully deafening. Trying to slow his traitorous racing heart, he awaited their verdict.

"It had better be, Professor Crowland, or it will be you on the firing line. Our clients require the greatest of discretion in their transactions, it would not bode well if it came to light who they were working with. Talking of clients, how are the upgrades coming along?"

A small sigh escaped the Professor's lips; a distraction was just what he needed. Trying to perk up, he spoke, "Yes well, as you know the previous specialist you sent me found several glitches in the new upgrades that they couldn't resolve, so I got Miles on the case and he has managed to resolve the conflicts with the integrations. We are currently testing and should be ready for production release imminently."

The so-called specialist they sent him was nothing more than a training monkey sent to spy and report back. He knew for a fact if they thought they could replicate his work without him he would be redundant in every sense of the word; he cringed thinking about its implications. Fortunately, he knew Miles was completely loyal to him, like the puppy he never wanted as a child. Focussing his attention back, they posed their next question.

"And what about the excess of the existing model, will there be much wastage?"

"Unfortunately, there will be some unavoidable wastage. Some may be salvageable for upgrade though, or at least used for testing, so wastage will be as limited as possible." He cringed at the thought of unnecessary waste, but a redundant product didn't have any place in the market. It was just product after all though, he knew he shouldn't let it bother him. As he pondered the most effective way to handle waste distribution, he was pulled from his thoughts once more.

"We want to know as soon as the missing product has been recovered and a full report on how this has happened. The new product line needs to be ready by the end of the month, so ensure you get your little assistant on it. Our clients don't like to be kept waiting. Remember, Professor Crowland, we gave you everything your little government-funded programme couldn't; we gave you the chance to make history, don't waste it."

Nodding, he thanked them once again for their support as he took his leave to return to the Institute. Stepping back out into the cooler air of the corridor, his shoulders relaxed and his whole body slumped as he loosened his tie. He had managed to stall for now but there was only so long he could give them the run around before they realised he didn't have a clue where it was… yet. He just prayed that Morgan didn't have a clue either, because if Morgan and that damned taskforce knew anything, they could become an issue. He knew he should have killed Morgan when he'd had the chance.

Three: Mairi

As my body relaxed, there came a knock at the door. I froze. This was becoming too much of an occurrence today. The knock came again, followed by the guy's voice.

"I know you're in there. They've gone, I promise."

Knife pulled behind my back, towel still wrapped securely, I cracked the door open slightly. He was indeed alone. I allowed him to enter and as soon as he was in I closed the door, pinning him against it with my knife firmly to his throat.

"Whoa! I just covered for you. No need to get violent." He stayed perfectly still not wanting to risk slipping against the blade.

"Who are you and what do you want?" I put it bluntly. He was obviously up to something; people didn't help strangers without an ulterior motive, so I tried to keep a stern face and my hand steady. I needed to maintain control.

"I was sent to help! Honestly, I knew who you were as soon as you arrived. I'm only here to help, I promise." His eyes weren't lying.

They say the eyes are the windows to the soul; well I'm not sure if that's true but I could tell when people were lying, it came naturally for as long as I could remember.

I still didn't trust him though.

"Talk quickly, before I change my mind," I said while releasing him from the grip of my knife and taking half a step back, hands still clenched to conceal the tremors.

He sat in the chair behind the door as I sat cautiously on the corner of the bed, the towel still wrapped tightly and the knife loosely held in my hand. He glanced at the blade and rubbed his hand across his neck where it had been only moments ago, "I was told you were coming and that I was to help you." I looked at him suspiciously

"Who told you, and help how?"

He sighed, "I can't tell you yet; it's not safe. But the people that I… well the people that I represent want to help you. You're being tracked and you don't know how? Well I can help with that too, but it needs to be done quickly before they realise I've sent them on a wild goose chase and come back here looking for us both."

"Why would you want to help me? And tracking, how?" I was getting very fidgety. It had been a long time since I'd had a chat with anyone past the necessary few words. I had already stayed here too long as it was and my skin was starting to crawl and my body was twitching. Discretely chewing the inside of my mouth, I tried to hide my unease.

"You are part of something much bigger than you realise. We have been tracking you for some time too and it's been discovered that back in their control you would be a danger to us all. They have been tracking you using an implant that was inserted the last time they had you in their possession."

Control; it was such a simple word that had such an impact throughout my life. Control over my life, the control others had over me and the control I had over others. Control was power and power meant survival. I've always been a survivor, somehow, with no other choice than to take control. But it wasn't what I wanted, none of this was what I wanted, I wasn't strong enough for any of it.

The way he said, 'the last time they had you in their possession,' played over in my head; like I was a piece of property owned or bought and it made me shudder. He was right. To them I was nothing more than an asset, a valuable asset they couldn't afford to lose

"How do I get it out?" I pointed the knife in his direction so he knew I wasn't messing about. Not that I think he had any doubts about what I was capable of.

"I can cut it out if you lend me your knife; I know exactly where it is."

I laughed! Did he think I was an idiot?

"You tell me where it is and I'll cut it out myself, the knife stays with me." I had only survived this long by being cautious. No need to get stupid now. The most innocent, and weakest were often the most deceptive; I was living proof of that. Never underestimate anyone… ever.

"You won't be able to; it's in the back of your neck. I am just here to help you, so why won't you let me help?"

I snapped. Launching towards him I straddled his lap, knife once again against his throat, I whispered in his ear with a hiss through gritted teeth, "Why on earth would I trust you, a person I know nothing about, to stand behind me with a knife and cut my flesh open? Does that sound logical to you?" I breathed softly into his ear, with the knife still poised so he got the gravity of his position. His body was trembling underneath mine, his legs weak and his breathing erratic.

He managed to stutter, "No, it's not logical, but waiting here to be caught is just plain stupid. You don't have to trust me, but you do need my help if you ever want to stop looking over your shoulder."

He paused as he glanced round the room, then said, "We could do it facing the mirror, that way you can see what I'm doing, how about that?"

I thought for a second before getting off his lap and beckoning him up. "One wrong move and I will snap your neck without a second thought, and if you know me like you say you do, you know I won't hesitate."

I think he got the message as he nodded with a gulp, standing slowly as I moved in front of the mirror, not wanting to give him the blade until I absolutely had to. Gripping the towel around my now dry body, I waited until we were both in front of the mirror before slowly passing him the knife over my shoulder. Bile threatened to emerge once more. Gritting my teeth and never taking my eyes off him, I watched as his body shook, holding the blade as if it were toxic.

"This may hurt, I apologise but I'll be as quick as I can."

I scoffed; I doubt he even knew the meaning of pain. I braced myself in preparation, gripping the material of the towel as the dull ache still emanated from my self-prescribed medical care earlier. He ran his fingers softly around the tops of my shoulder blades with a delicate touch that tickled as his fingers brushed along my skin. My eyes closed momentarily as I shivered. Once he'd found the spot he was looking for, he pressed firmly around before speaking.

"You ready?" he said as I nodded. Still gritting my teeth, my eyes locked on him in the mirror's reflection as I saw concern plastered across his face. He slowly pierced the skin between my shoulder blades and I could feel the pressure across my upper back as the knife broke the skin and pushed through into the muscle below. Deeper and deeper, the pain multiplied as my nerve endings realised what was going on, searing down my spine as my body screamed for me to stop. I didn't move as my body froze in shock, refusing to take my eyes off him as a traitorous tear rolled down my cheek. My legs began trembling and as the shock wore off and the pain became sharper, I focussed on my reflection. My face was a picture of stone and I needed it to stay that way. The lie, that mask I wore to protect myself. I wasn't sure if I even knew who the real me was but I prayed it wasn't the cold face staring back from the mirror; my heart told me it couldn't be, could it?

He noticed the tear that had now become several trickles before I could wipe it away. "I'm sorry," he said, "I'll be as quick as I can. This next bit may be uncomfortable."

Not sure what he meant, I braced myself for the worst but I was ill-prepared. Pulling the knife from the freshly created hole in my back he then placed his finger into the wound, pushing through the outer flesh and into the muscle. Spasms shot down my spine and my knees buckled without consent as my body ignored any instruction I gave it. What only took seconds felt like the whole world had stopped, trapped in that torturous moment. What I wouldn't have given for my autopilot to have taken the reins at that moment but she was nowhere to be seen, unusual for her.

As he pulled his finger back out I could see the culprit, my body still shaking as I tried to maintain what composure I had left, hoping he hadn't noticed.

So they had been tracking me and now it was gone. He took the tiny little device, smaller than a fingernail and flushed it down the toilet. "That should keep it moving for a while and keep them off our backs," he said, still holding my knife in his hand. Realising the look of discomfort on my face, he handed it back to me, handle first, smiling awkwardly.

"Let's get you patched up and dressed. I just need some supplies from my trolley outside the door. I nodded vaguely, my mind reeling, feeling vulnerable. I had to snap out of it. It wasn't an option, this wasn't the plan; not that there was a specific plan.

But I didn't need help; I stayed solitary. It kept me alive and kept everyone else alive too. My heart was still raw from the lessons I'd learnt about caring. It got people killed in the most gruesome of ways.

He returned moments later with a bag. He was still cautiously looking at me as if I were a ticking bomb, ready to explode. Maybe I was? Who knew? Out of the bag, he pulled clothes and a small wash bag. Opening it he pulled out bandages and an array of first aid supplies. Gesturing for me to sit, he approached slowly and began cleaning the open wound on my back. This whole interaction was the first time I had let someone else touch me in as long as I could remember. His gentle fingers gliding a wipe across the cut he had made, sending a tingle across the surface of my skin, followed by the delicate touch as he placed butterfly stitches across the open hole to seal the gap. Once done, he then moved on to my earlier wounds. He was just about to touch one when I flinched without meaning to, unsure of how to react.

"It's ok, I just want to help. Let me look."

I couldn't trust my voice not to betray me. Clinging to my towel and feeling very exposed, goosebumps started appearing across the tops of my arms. I watched as he attentively cleaned and bandaged each of the existing wounds before looking straight into my eyes.

I had a rule: Never make direct eye contact. It was easier to be forgotten if they hadn't looked into your soul. Too late. My wounds tended to, he handed me a neatly folded pile of fresh clothes.

"These should fit hopefully. I thought they may be better than what you arrived in."

Heading into the bathroom but not forgetting my blade, I glanced back at him; I hadn't completely lost my wits yet. Placing the blade on the side of the sink I dressed quickly and silently. Once clothed I considered the cracked mirror above the sink, hands either side leaning on the counter, with fatigue setting in as the adrenaline wore off. I looked at my reflection long and hard; something I usually avoided at all costs. Looking at myself meant judging and I wasn't ready to deal with the things I'd done to survive. A lump in my throat built up as my eyes started to water and I sniffled and wiped my face, splashing cold water across my flushed cheeks.

I'd locked those memories into a vault in my mind, refusing to access them and expose myself to the horrors I had witnessed. One day, maybe I would open it back up and face my demons but not today, it was an ongoing battle to maintain control but one I had no choice but to fight. No matter how terrified I was, the alternative was worse. Once I was as composed as I could muster, I exited the bathroom and returned to my new 'acquaintance.' He was wearing a pair of surgical gloves and was wiping all the surfaces in the room with a cloth, disposing of any trace we had ever been there. He had done this before. Looking up at me he stopped.

"Do they fit ok? I'm sorry if they're not the best but hopefully they will be comfy for you."

I nodded as he proceeded throughout the bathroom, bagging up my old blood-stained clothes from the sink and ensuring there were no remnants of us to trace.

"I'm afraid we need to get going just in case they circle back here. Are you ready?"

I hadn't travelled with anyone in years and hadn't trusted anyone for just as long, but here I was in this grotty room actually thinking about going with him. I mean I had been running for so long with no answers, no solutions and no plan. Could he possibly have the answers? Or was this just an elaborate trap I was walking into? What choice did I really have though? This wasn't living, it was barely surviving and my will to continue was starting to tire.

"I suppose I don't have a choice, but if I even sniff something's off I'm gone, you hear me?" He nodded. His eyes seemed quite sincere, but I kept him at a suitably safe distance. Zipping the jacket up and pulling the hood firmly over my face, I followed him out the door with my head down but eyes scanning for any movement. There was an eerie silence, with nobody about that I could see except my acquaintance and me.

Four: Mairi

Heading through the empty car park we approached a car, muted in colour and neither new nor old. It didn't stand out and I couldn't even tell which make it was. It had four doors and four wheels, that was all I could remember, which I presume was intentional. Looking around to check we hadn't been followed, we both got into the front seats.

I pulled my seat belt on slowly, ensuring I did nothing to stand out. Doing the same, he started the engine; the low rumbling of the radio and the heater blowing quietly. I heard the click of the headlights as we began to move. An awkward silence built up, until at last he broke it, "How rude of me, I forgot to introduce myself; my name is Bram," he smiled.

How could someone dragged into all of this still manage such a carefree smile? I tried an awkward smile back, but it felt so uncomfortable. I envied him and his stupid smile.

"I'm… I mean my name is Mairi."

"Yes, I already know," he said calmly. How stupid of me, he knew where to find me so obviously he would know my name. Enter the return of the awkward silence and the buzzing of the slightly out-of-tune radio.

My mind drifted as I gazed out of the window. It was dark outside but the passing streetlamps gave me glimpses of the scenery along the route. It had been a while since I'd travelled in such luxury; I was usually walking or hitching rides in the back of unsuspecting vehicles, trying to be invisible as I ran as fast as I could.

Thinking of what it would be like to have a normal life, I hugged my arms around my torso. I couldn't even picture a dream in my head. Snatches of memories from before were the most I could manage. Fleeting flashes of my mother's beautiful face. No. It was too painful.

As we cruised smoothly down the dual carriageway, my new acquaintance began to indicate left. We slowed and turned off the main road onto a single road through an iron gate. I could see lots of shipping containers. It seemed like we were in a storage yard of some kind, possibly near the docks as the ports to oil rigs were dotted about all across the coastline. I'd thought about trying to get on them several times, but it meant no escape if they found me there and I didn't fancy my chances in the sea. He drove on, seemingly knowing where he was going as we headed further and further from the main road and the protection of the streetlamps fading in the distance.

The darkness encircled us as the light disappeared behind. The car began to slow near a small electricity substation, surrounded by its metal fencing and its warning signs of death by high voltage. I couldn't understand why we were slowing; there was nothing here. Maybe I'd made a big mistake? My hand clenched around the blade once more as I prepared myself for an ambush.

"We're here," he said, his tone still light.

"And where is here?" I replied coldly. He didn't answer my question but instead headed towards the tiny little substation and opened the gate, looking around to make sure nobody was nearby before he beckoned me to follow. Since when did I follow anyone into buildings in dark abandoned storage yards? I must have finally gone over the edge, because before I knew it I was following him in through the gates. Pulling a key from his pocket he unlocked the door. What on earth were we doing at a shed? I couldn't work out how there were any answers here. My heart was racing and my mind was in overdrive, I was ready to run and every part of my body screamed at me, but instead I followed him inside. He locked the door behind us, alarm bells ringing even louder in my head. It was pitch black in the small building so he pulled out a torch and lit the room. It looked just as I thought it should; large metal boxes lining the walls with thick wires leading out and into the ground. No windows or other doors, just the small room around us. He was staring at the floor looking for something.

I was losing my patience as I said, "Look, what is going on? I don't really think you know who you're messing with."

I'd never actually hurt an unarmed man, but he didn't know that. He wasn't listening to me as he ran his fingers across the floor. I thought he had dropped something, but then, as if he'd found what he was looking for, he began to pull at the floor revealing a manhole leading downwards. He flashed the torch down the hole and I could see a set of ladders attached to the side.

"You'll need to go first so I can close the entrance afterwards. Here's the torch so you can see where you're going," he said as he passed the torch to my empty hand.

I looked at the torch in my one hand and the blade in my other, weighing up my options. I placed the torch in my mouth and the blade in my back pocket as I descended the cold metal ladder to what I expected to be a sewer of some kind.

Five: Morgan

Sitting at her desk anxiously, Morgan took off her glasses and ran her fingers through the fiery strands of hair that smoothly flowed through her hands and back into place. She had been expecting a report hours ago. Intel had come in that the package had been located, so what was taking so long? It was killing her just sitting here, she couldn't take the suspense.

Checking in with head office again, they hadn't heard anything, or at least not anything they were willing to divulge. Red tape and more red tape on top, the joys of working for the government; but she didn't expect anything different. You had a set of rules you had to play by, or at least pretend to; it was the only way to keep the suits happy.

Their enemies had always been one step ahead, but they still couldn't work out how. She had suspected a leak, but each one of her team had come directly from the government programmes, vetted, screened and scrutinised under a microscope. She knew every single detail of their lives right down to their granny's secret soup recipes. But they were managing somehow and blocking her from making any progress at every turn so far.

She knew they needed results fast; the task force was running out of time and if they didn't have a break soon, the funding would be pulled and the GAP taskforce would be no more. All those years of looking and searching would be for nothing and she would still be left with unanswered questions.

No, there was no point thinking that way. Her agent was on the job; failure was not an option. She just needed to have more patience; they would update her as soon as they could. If they *could* update. The worry continued to spread as she played every gruesome scenario through her mind.

The cool confidence and exterior she wore was her armour. It made her an effective leader and although she had no real friends, she was well respected and her team was loyal to a fault. If only her team had seen her all those years ago, when she was first given the taskforce.

Young, naive and meek, with no leadership skills or experience she had bumbled into her office that first day so flustered and nervous. But there was one thing that hadn't changed: her mission. Nothing on this Earth would come between her and her mission.

She had quickly learned and adapted. Surrounding herself with some of the youngest talent from each department, all fresh from the academy and eager to start. Everyone had said she was mad, taking on such a young inexperienced team, but she proved them all wrong and all these years later she had the most loyal, specialised team in any department. Met with the highest success record in all its missions, except one. The one they had been created for. But the mission wasn't over yet.

If the package could be found it would be the break she needed. That one breadcrumb to start the trail back to the shadows who were pulling the strings in the darkness where she could end this once and for all.

Every lead so far had led to nothing, with whispers of rumours and wisps of smoke, most thought she may have well been chasing a ghost. But this, this was different. It was a real, tangible, physical piece of evidence. If their source was right, this could unravel everything and bring her the results she had been chasing for so many years. The head of the real monster.

Her computer pinged. She shot up, shoving her glasses back on and checking her screen. She slumped back into the chair. Not the information she was hoping for, just an email from higher up requesting yet more paperwork for a meeting about a meeting. She sighed, thinking of the bigger picture and not the cage she was currently pacing.

This was the only way; she needed them to help her retrieve the package and finish things once and for all. Taking a deep breath, she began filling out the request with the hope it would help to pass the time while she waited for her update.

A small blonde head popped around the corner of her door as she looked up expectantly. She realised with a hint of disappointment it was just her PA, Aileana.

"Would you like a cup of... ma'am?"

"I'd love something stronger but I'm sure there's a policy somewhere against it, so I suppose tea will be fine, thank you Aileana."

Aileana smiled softly. She was such a gentle soul, a very calming influence but extremely good at her job and she could organise anything in her sleep. Morgan looked up thoughtfully at her and said, "Aileana, the operative we lost last month, what was the cover story that went out to the family?"

Aileana checked her tablet, scrolling through before looking up. "Gas explosion in the office ma'am, a tragic but unfortunate accident. The family have been awarded compensation and the funeral arrangements have been taken care of. Do you need me to put out a new advert for a replacement?"

Morgan paused for a moment, she wasn't in the mood for training up fresh blood, but she couldn't afford to be an operative down as the one they had lost had been her best language specialist.

"Yes," she said as she pinched the bridge of her nose, "put an advert out for a languages specialist for one-to-one tuition in various locations, with only GAP students applicable to apply." She was required to advertise publicly for all roles as they were funded by the government and all wage bills had to be traceable. The real role, however, technically never existed and all operatives were given a cover story for their new jobs.

"Ensure you send the advert straight to the academy as well. I want their top five candidates; they know my preferences."

Aileana, tapping like mad on her tablet nodding repeatedly before looking up like she'd forgotten something. "Oh, and I thought you'd like to know he's returned; I think possibly with what you were looking for," she said, smiling sweetly as Morgan fussed around neatening up her desk furiously.

"Get him to come and see me as soon as he's ready, we haven't got any time to lose."

Aileana nodded politely as she took her leave and headed out towards the kitchen area. As she turned out of the door she bumped into a figure loitering nearby, dropping the contents of her arms across the floor. Apologetically, the cause of the collision helped to pick up the files as Aileana distractedly looked over her tablet with panic to check it wasn't damaged. The nervous wreck in front of her started rambling.

"I'm so sorry, I was sent to see you, or at least I think you… I didn't want to disturb you but I didn't want to get lost again, and now I'm rambling! I'm Cora, the new intern." Cora stood nervously showing her ID badge. Aileana couldn't remember a new intern starting but they sent her so many of them and none tended to last long with the boss's high expectations, she beckoned Cora to follow. Aileana had a feeling it was going to be a long day.

Composing herself, Morgan rearranged her red locks again while straightening her glasses and shoving the excess paperwork into her top drawer and out of sight. Silently, she prayed this was the break she needed. If this was the missing link she had been waiting for then the real hard work was just about to begin.

Six: Mairi

What I was faced with as I descended the ladder was entirely different to any expectations I could have had. Stepping off the bottom rung, I was met with people rushing up and down a well-lit corridor; none bothered by my arrival, some glancing and smiling as they passed and some too busy to even notice me. I took in the well-lit space that reminded me of a hospital; very clinical and clean with intelligent-looking people holding clipboards and bustling about. I heard the footsteps of what I presumed was Bram coming down the ladder behind me. He hopped down with a spring in his step.

"Feels good to be home," he said. "Let's go find Morgan and introduce you."

Very much feeling like the odd one out, I followed silently while taking in the layout, the doors and any points of interest for a viable escape route if needed. There was no security and nobody seemed to be armed but the surveillance and technology suggested to me this wasn't your local community hospital.

Keeping up at a trot I asked, "So then, who's Morgan? Is he the one who's got all the answers?"

Answers; I'd given up even believing I would find them. I was simply just trying to survive, until he arrived, dressed in his loose jeans and trainers with his mop of hair. We entered a small kitchen area and he gestured for me to sit before making me a cup of sweet tea.

"You look like you need it," he said with a smile, "I'll be back in a moment, I just need to change." Before I could even question how he knew how I liked my tea, he was gone.

I cupped the mug in my hands, relishing the warmth against my fingers. As I sipped the hot liquid, it filtered down my throat like a taste of heaven. It had been a while since I'd had the luxury of sitting and enjoying a hot drink. A picture of hot chocolate flashed across my mind and I shuddered, blocking it out when I realised where the memory was from.

Moments later he returned, transformed. The chilled-out surfer was gone, replaced by a smart look but with the same smile and honest eyes. He was now wearing spectacles, a fitted black top and smart jeans, the look completed with a cardigan that suggested it belonged to a schoolteacher. I stared a little longer than I should have before returning my gaze to my tea.

"Morgan's ready to see you," he said with a bright smile. His smile was quite infectious, although I resisted catching it as he led me from the small kitchen still clutching my tea with both hands and my knife poking me slightly where I had placed it for security, thinking I really should get a knife holder or something. I'd lose fewer jeans that way, but oh well, hindsight was a glorious thing.

We entered an office, clean and clinical just like the rest of wherever we were, and in an official-looking chair behind a desk sat a well dressed woman. She looked like she belonged in a corner office in a posh company. She was in her early forties with fiery, red hair that sat perfectly. She looked up from her desk, taking her glasses off she softly spoke, "You must be Mairi. I hear you're looking for some answers."

Straight to the point. "You must be Morgan?" I asked. She nodded.

"I think we need to have a chat, we've much to discuss and time is precious."

Of course, she'd have questions for me too. But did she know what she was asking of me? Was it a can of worms I was capable of opening? More importantly, could I wash the blood off my hands afterwards?

I had a feeling it was going to be a long night. I sat down wearily at the desk, pulling my knife out of my pocket and placing it gently in front of me next to the tea and asked, "So where do we start?"

"At the beginning, of course, I need to know everything to be able to give you all the answers you need and a possible way forward."

Seven: Mairi

The beginning was a lifetime ago, so much had changed. I shifted uncomfortably, feeling overly warm as my hands started clamming up. I wasn't sure how to proceed. Sensing my unease Morgan spoke again. "OK, how about I start with what I know and you can help me fill in the gaps?" she suggested.

She was straight to the point, but her tone wasn't rude and it made me feel comfortable, which in turn made me feel even more uneasy as my ankles crossed each other and I tensed my legs to stop them twitching. Nodding, I sat biding my time to see where the path took me. She looked at me intently, like a puzzle to solve, and continued to talk.

"So, what we do know is that you weren't your mother's biological child."

I cringed thinking about my mother.

"You were found abandoned at a church with no information and your mother took you in."

I nodded, it was all correct and my mother had never hidden the truth from me.

"As a child, you were bright, an all-round successful student." Morgan stopped to take a brief sip from her glass, adjusting her glasses as she continued, "Then, they came to your home. Your mother believed them to be a government-funded programme for the gifted and talented. They offered you the scholarship programme that many would dream of and of course your mother signed you up right away. Only it wasn't a government programme, in fact it was something else entirely and when you finally realised, you escaped. The first ever to do so." She paused.

"That's about all the facts we have, however we don't think you were abandoned as a baby; we believe you were planted. Inserted into an environment until they were ready to collect you." She stared at me, awaiting a response. But all I could manage was silence.

My brain spinning, I glanced around the room before my eyes met Morgan's. "Did my mother know?" I asked but I wasn't sure if I wanted to know the answer.

Morgan shook her head and a relieved breath escaped my lips. "No, we don't think so. We believe she was just another victim, like you."

Victim. Is that the word that was used? I didn't have words to describe what happened that day. I didn't need to, the images were seared into my brain like a movie playing on repeat that I could never turn off. When I escaped, I was still naïve and confused and just like any child who felt lost I returned straight to the place I felt safest; home. It will always be my biggest regret, one that will haunt me forever. My soul had been destroyed that day.

The room was uncomfortably quiet, before I knew what I was doing my lips had already started moving, "I didn't feel any different to any of my friends at school. I was able to hold my own in most areas of my schooling but nothing special, so when they turned up it was a complete shock."

My throat felt dry, so I accepted the glass of water offered to me by Bram who had been standing by the door the entire time, listening to the exchange. He looked like he wanted to speak but refrained, so I turned back to Morgan and continued, staring at the glass as if it was the most interesting thing in the world.

Eight: Mairi

"First week of the school holidays I was really excited about all the things mum and I had planned, I was plotting on my map all the places we were going to visit when someone knocked at the door. Mum went to answer and I heard her talking to someone. She beckoned me into the living room and I sat next to her, the lady and gentleman sat opposite. I didn't like the feel of them but Mum said that was because she'd taught me to always be wary of strangers."

It had been a long time since I had spoken about my mother or even said the word mum aloud. The word was like a jagged rock lodged in my throat every time I tried to say it. It was the hardest thing I'd ever had to do. It still didn't feel real.

"They introduced themselves as representatives from the 'Institute' for the gifted, a government-led initiative to identify and nurture talented children. They weren't specific on the exact location. Apparently, I had been nominated for a place by my school. They talked to us for a while about a scholarship programme that I had been accepted for."

I took a deep breath before continuing, "After they had gone, my mum immediately contacted the school who confirmed the story. She researched them online and they seemed to check out, it all just seemed too good to be true. We should have known it was."

Morgan's expression was unreadable, there was no betraying what was going on behind those golden orbs staring intently at me. She didn't speak, but instead nodded for me to continue.

"The next few weeks were a bit of a blur, my mum seemed like she'd won the lottery. She was buying me new clothes and packing everything except the kitchen sink. Although, I think she would have packed that too if she thought it would have fit. I couldn't remember ever seeing her so excited as those weeks leading up to me leaving; not because I was leaving but simply because she felt I was getting an opportunity she would have never been able to offer me. Well, she wasn't wrong there, I suppose."

Those few weeks with Mum had been some of my happiest memories, we went on so many days out. I could tell she was trying to cherish every moment with me before she let me go. I can still remember how it felt to have her arms wrapped around me, her warm smile and that delicate kiss on my forehead as she reminded me how much she loved me. My lip began to quiver as I gripped the glass tighter, but the tug on my heart could not be ignored no matter how much I tried to lie to myself. I glanced up but then away from Morgan's intense gaze to refocus, blinking repeatedly until I could continue

"The morning came for me to go; my mum had offered to take me there but they came up with numerous reasons why it would be better for them to collect me. Looking back, we should have seen then that something wasn't quite right, but that glow from my mum prevented me from looking past her excitement."

Morgan interrupted sensing my need for a break, "And so they came and took you and you willingly went thinking nothing was amiss? Did you suspect anything at all at this point?"

I wasn't sure if it was a question or an accusation but as I thought about it, I knew deep down that something hadn't felt right. I hadn't wanted to go, but I couldn't bear to risk disappointing my mother, so I pushed the doubts down and smiled as I waved her goodbye. I looked at Morgan, nodding my head and quietly replying, "Yes, but I thought it was just nerves about leaving mum so I shook it off and didn't say anything… I should have said something."

Morgan reached out to me, placing her hand on mine. I jumped, pulling away startled before realizing that she was trying to comfort me. I slowly placed my hand back apprehensively and looked at the woman before me.

"Never blame yourself, you were a child. You still are."

"I haven't been a child for a very long time," I replied simply. It wasn't a statement; it was an unfortunate fact. Childhood was a distant memory belonging to another person I didn't think even existed anymore.

"The school was beautiful. I can't remember much of the journey there no matter how much I try, it all felt quite… hazy." Morgan's expression changed slightly, but only for a passing moment as she scribbled something on a post-it note while nodding at me to continue.

"But I do remember pulling up, it was an impressive sight. Reminded me of those stately homes you see in the movies." I remember how nervous I was but at the time I thought it was natural when starting a new adventure. Looking back, I should have seen it was my instincts screaming something was horribly wrong.

A shudder ran down my spine and I felt a hand on my shoulder. As I glanced up Bram was there, words weren't needed. The encouragement of his hand calmed me, which was a feeling I hadn't felt in a very long time. I sniffled, wiping a hand across my nose.

"School was, well, amazing. My days were perfect and my friends were lovely. My teachers were all fantastic, the weather was always great and I always slept like a baby."

Morgan made eye contact and said, "Sounds a little too perfect."

"It was," I replied

Even now, trying to think back to memories I knew were there, I couldn't remember the individual details. I knew my teachers were lovely but I couldn't picture their faces. I knew I was enjoying myself but I couldn't recall the sounds of laughter from all the fun. I knew the food was always my favourite thing but I couldn't bring back the taste or the smell to trigger the memories.

"I don't have a bad memory from those early days, but the more I try to think of the details the hazier it becomes," I said as looked into my glass intently.

Morgan nodded again, scribbling down a messy set of notes; I doubted she could even read them herself. As she was about to continue speaking the world began to spin and every fibre of my being screamed at me, right down to the hairs on my body standing on end. I didn't know what was going on but I knew it wasn't cake and tea on its way.

Figures started dashing up and down the halls and one popped a blonde head through the door. Three words were all she spoke

"Code Yellow ma'am," she said and without another word, she left.

Morgan pulled her USB drive from her computer and grabbed the notes she had been making before nodding to Bram. Glancing down at me she said, "We'll pick up this conversation later Mairi. I'll be seeing you again soon," before she left with a hasty stride.

Feeling like a lost sheep, I tried to work out what was going on. The speed of bodies dashing about indicated it wasn't anything good. I looked to Bram for an explanation.

"We need to get going, we haven't much time. I'll explain en route," he said, gently rousing me from the chair.

I snatched my knife from the table, confused and shaky. I wanted answers and I wanted them immediately. I could have forced him to explain, but something was telling me getting out of there was more of a priority.

Nine: Mairi

I followed Bram silently down the clinical hallways, the corridors filled with bodies rushing in every direction. There wasn't a panicked stampede but they were all focused and driven, far from the friendly atmosphere I had arrived to earlier. We weaved down several corridors, each one seemingly identical to the next. Not running but moving at a brisk pace.

He kept glancing back at me, looking at me like he had at the bed and breakfast as if I was something unstable. As we turned down yet another corridor, there was a voice over the speaker system which bellowed two simple words.

"Code White."

"What does that mean Bram? What is going on? I want answers or I'm going no further." I knew we didn't have time, but I'd survived this long by having my wits about me and now I didn't even have a clue where the hell I was. I could feel myself becoming more and more on edge. It was never a good sign.

"We'll walk and talk but we need to keep moving," he urged, grabbing my hand to pull me with him.

BIG mistake. In one swift move, I had pulled round and had him backed against the wall with my knife against his throat, a low growl emitting from me. I had no control when the instincts kicked in and the end result was usually not very sunny for whoever set them off, but by the skin of my teeth I had managed to pull myself back. I stood there breathing heavily with the knife still against his neck and a hand still securely round his wrist.

He didn't move, he didn't speak, he just looked. He stared and waited. I don't know whether he was sure I wouldn't hurt him, or if he was just silently praying, but he didn't resist or move. I could have ended him there. I still don't know to this day how I had stopped myself. Maybe it was the fact he didn't try to fight that made my instinct back down but either way, whatever occurred did so with impeccable timing.

For what must have been seconds, but felt like a lifetime, we stood there. Our eyes were locked as the knife was still held in place. I breathed out and carefully stepped back, removing the blade as a red trickle rolled down his neck.

"Don't. Ever. Grab. Me. Again. You might not be so lucky next time."

He didn't reply, but instead held his hand out, offering it to me like a gift.

I had almost killed the guy and yet he stood right there in front of me open-handed, as if offering to help me cross the road. Maybe he was crazier than he looked. I apprehensively took his hand and allowed him to guide me onwards, quickly resuming our pace.

"Don't think this gets you out of answers," I piped up after a few moments. I could have sworn I heard him chuckle, but I couldn't see his face.

He spoke, not looking back, "We need to relocate and regroup with Morgan. We have some unwanted visitors on the way."

A cold chill swept over me, they'd found me. Somehow, they had still managed to track me. I'd led them here to all these poor people, endangering everyone. My heart was racing and panic was setting in. Not for myself, but for the possible danger I had put so many others in.

"We're nearly at the far exit, then we will need to get some distance from here," Bram continued. "We're not quite sure how anyone found this location yet so we'll have to lay low until we work out what's happened."

The corridors were now empty, we had not passed another person since our slight 'delay' in the previous corridor. As we approached the door ahead I could hear footsteps, but there was something off about them.

"Bram, something's not right," I said as I tried to pull him back.

He glanced at me and then ahead before saying, "It's the only way out I'm afraid."

The door ahead moved, creaking slightly as the outline of a figure pushed against it. Bram ran towards the door before I could stop him and as I followed I could see him dragging a figure back through the door. I instantly recognized the face, it was the woman who had brought the Code Yellow earlier.

I heard him whisper, "Shhh Aileana, it's ok, I've got you."

Her face was pale and her clothes were blood-soaked but I couldn't tell where it was originating from. Bram was desperately talking to her in reassuring tones.

I tried to think of how best to help her, but I was only experienced in causing pain not fixing it. I took my jacket off, rolling it up to support her head and Bram glanced at me nodding as he opened her shirt to try and locate the source of the blood. Her breathing was shallow and laboured and though I knew this was a pointless effort, I couldn't help but try and at least seem to be doing something to stop the inevitable.

As he tried to stem the tide of blood, she was desperately trying to tell us something. I couldn't work out what she was trying to say but Bram hushed her, telling her to save her energy as he pressed down. She was bleeding out faster than a leaky bucket and, as I expected, within moments she had taken her last breath.

Drenched in her blood, Bram's head drooped at the realization. He pulled himself to his feet looking defeated before he quietly said, "We need to keep moving."

I looked down at the body before my feet, her lifeless eyes still open and staring into nothingness, void of all. I gently leant down and carefully closed her eyes, hoping that peace had found her swiftly, unlike whoever had done this.

He tapped my arm, silently indicating towards the door. That door that held death in its wake, waiting to capture more souls beyond. Whatever Aileana had been trying to warn us about, it was too late. We were walking straight into it. I just hoped they were ready for what they were about to get.

A calm wave descended over me; a familiar feeling of detachment, like I was there but not there at the same time. It was comforting in a strange way. I pushed Bram behind me and entered swiftly through the doors, making my grand entrance into the playground ahead.

Ten: Mairi

They descended as I crossed the threshold of the door. No wonder the poor woman hadn't stood a chance, but now they were dealing with me and I had a feeling they hadn't a clue what they were getting themselves into.

A daze took over me like I was floating, time slowed as I gracefully danced with my blade in hand, creating a work of art filled with reds of every shade. There was no mercy, no swift release. They would remember my face seared into their memories as I sent them to the next life screaming for the end.

I vaguely heard the crack of bone as a leg snapped clean through his clothes, you could see the shards of bone protruding as he tried to drag himself away. Pathetic excuse of a man, trying to desperately save himself.

I approached slowly, there was no rush and he wasn't going anywhere. He was backed into a corner, desperately looking around and weighing up his options. I saw him glance at each of the bodies around him, his fallen comrades who had failed to present a challenge before being dispatched. I loomed over him as I heard him begging. I couldn't make out the muffled words but the tones were the familiar ones of a desperate soul willing to say anything to keep a few more precious moments on this Earth.

He tried to reason with me, to appeal to my conscience. She, however, was currently locked away in the vaults of my mind; it was safer that way, for her sake and mine. Emotion was a needless distraction that provided weakness at times like this, the reason I was here and she was not.

I loomed over the blubbering excuse, currently crying and possibly soiling himself if the smells were anything to go by. I raised my blade for the final dance but as I was about to deal the final blow, I felt a hand stop me.

I spun around and met Bram's eyes. Was this guy an idiot? Had he not learned anything?! He was talking but his voice was muffled and distant. His eyes though, they were as clear as a summer's day.

I froze, my heart began to slow and I blinked once, twice. The world came back into focus, as his voice became clearer. "We need information; we need him alive," he stated.

"If you hadn't noticed, I don't do alive very well," I said, my breath bated as I took back the reins. It hadn't been one of my strongest points over the last few years. I was definitely back in the room and the sight around me was causing my body to shake.

"Let me handle this, you keep watch." He didn't demand or question; did he know? But he asked in such a way I complied without objection, trying not to look at my handy work; I wasn't sure my stomach could handle it.

I scanned the perimeter for any other threats, treading carefully around the recently deceased men that littered the floor. Bram was leant over our new friend quietly talking to him in tones I couldn't quite hear. A moment later he stood, then bending over the guy promptly took his head in both hands and followed it with a swift CRACK. The guy didn't even have time to react. My heart jumped at the sound still echoing in my ears.

So, he wasn't as innocent as he looked.

"Well, did you get anything?" I asked impatiently, trying not to show my discomfort.

"No, just garbled rubbish that didn't make sense."

I didn't believe him but I didn't push the issue, instead following him towards the exit and the welcoming breeze outside.

The silence was deafening, with not a living soul in sight. Or so I thought.

A muffled noise came from behind the nearest vehicle. I gestured to Bram and we cautiously approached from either side.

Step by step we snuck closer until the figure came into sight. It was a woman, huddled down behind the wheel trying desperately to hide. She must have escaped the welcoming party we encountered, a very lucky escape for her indeed. I noticed an ID badge dangling and I could just about make out the name: Cora.

She asked where the men were, obviously distressed and worried for her safety.

"Don't worry Cora," I tried reassuring her, "they won't be bothering anyone anymore."

I expected to see relief flood across her, but instead I saw a flash of something entirely different, almost like panic. I glanced to Bram, who had also noticed the exchange and we both looked at her. She gulped, backing herself further against the wheel.

"It was you!" I didn't need confirmation, her face said it all. Backing away in horror, the image of Aileana flashed before my eyes.

Bram rounded in on her speaking softly, but with a dangerous undertone, "Tell me everything." It wasn't a request.

"I can't," she stuttered, "they'll kill me."

I looked her square in the eye, "And you think I won't?"

Horror flashed across her face as she realized the impossible situation her betrayal had put her in. "You don't understand, they'll hurt my family. They know everything, they are everywhere," she said as her eyes frantically glanced round as if we were being watched.

Bram spoke again with no compassion in his tone, "Who are they? I won't ask again."

She pulled something from her pocket and before we could react she stabbed herself in the leg. Her body started violently convulsing, her eyes rolled back and her mouth frothed as the poison took effect. She slumped. Gone. And with her went any answers.

Bram, filled with frustration kicked the wheel her body was slumped against, causing the body to slip to the floor with a dull thud.

"So now we know how our visitors found us and we're still as clueless as blind mice," he moaned to nobody in particular.

"Well not exactly, we now know you had a leak, which means we know we can't trust anyone." In my head it read *I* can't trust anyone but I didn't want to raise suspicion with him yet. Always expect the worst. It had kept me alive this long.

Eleven: Mairi

We made haste to avoid any more unwanted visitors, finding the nearest car and putting as much space in between us and any pursuers as possible. Bram drove, apparently not trusting me to. It wasn't my fault I didn't have a license; I was still a far better driver than him.

As we drove down the dimly lit roads, I sat thinking, barely aware of the buzzing of the radio or the humming of the heater. My eyes drooping as the adrenaline wore off, tiredness consuming my body as the warmth flooded over me and the darkness welcomed me to the sandman.

***

My eyes shot open but I couldn't see, panic set in as I tried to move but couldn't. Completely restrained, I thrashed about desperately trying to loosen my bonds. Blinking repeatedly, I realised I couldn't see for the cloth bag over my head, stifling my breath and causing the hot air emanating from my mouth to rapidly overheat my face.

My heart galloped as I tried to work out what had happened. I had escaped with Bram; we were in the car. That was the last thing I remembered. Everything after that was a complete blank.

My brain started running through every possible scenario: Had we been ambushed? Had we been attacked? Or worse still, were my secret suspicions confirmed? Had he betrayed me? But why help me escape and let his accomplices die if he was a traitor? What the hell was going on?

I could hear footsteps, and voices exchanging words. Those voices, they seemed somehow… familiar.

NO! If I was panicked before it was nothing to the wave of terror that flooded over me as the realisation dawned as to where I was. My bladder threatened to give way as my body betrayed me in fear.

The footsteps grew closer and as I felt a hand tug at the cloth, I was blinded by the harsh lights. Blinking, my eyes struggled to adjust as I saw the outlines of the figures surrounding me. I'd been transported back to hell.

I'd woken up here before in this exact same room, with these exact same people. The horror of the memories overwhelmed me as I gasped and struggled to breathe. It had been months, but suddenly only felt like seconds. I tried to speak but no words would escape my lips.

They bustled around me, talking with each other without even acknowledging me; like I wasn't even there. But I was, and it wasn't good. It never was.

After they'd filled in various forms and looked at the multitude of machines currently attached to me, they vacated the room without a word, leaving me alone and stranded. I wasn't even able to scratch my nose.

Time to go, I wasn't prepared for a repeat performance of my last experience here. I still had the scars both mental and physical.

As the footsteps dissipated, I took a deep breath. It was now or never.

My wrists and ankles were sore and bloody from struggling against my restraints, my flesh raw as it grated against the harsh cuffs. Time for a new strategy: A drastic one. Closing my eyes, I slowed my breathing and became as calm as I could. Then, gritting my teeth in anticipation, I wiggled my thumb ready and... POP.

The pain flooded through me, but the fear pushed it back down as I concentrated on pulling my now mangled hand free from its confines. Now the hard part. It was always harder putting the thumb back. *1, 2, 3... CRUNCH.*

Argh, that was always more painful than I remembered.

Quickly bringing myself to my senses, I released the other three restraints with my now free, if slightly sore, hand and then ripped the numerous tubes and wires attached to me out with one swift tug. I knew where I had to go and I knew I was running out of time.

Cracking the door open, I peeked out and saw two figures chatting. I pulled myself back in and crouched down below the door, waiting for them to pass and praying for them not to enter. I didn't want to alert anyone this early on.

As they had passed I snuck another glance. The coast was clear.

Dressed in some sort of scrubs, I looked down at my feet. No shoes; that always made it more difficult to move quickly. I made a dash for the corridor, keeping low and moving as silently as possible. Swiftly, I managed to clear several corridors with ease.

As I approached the next door, it swung open and two figures exited with clipboards in hand. I breathed in and flattened myself against the wall, not that it would shield me but by some luck they walked in the opposite direction without a glance back. I snuck into the room they had vacated whilst I waited for another opportune moment to further my escape.

As I entered the room, I realised it was a room I hadn't encountered on my last visit. At first glance it seemed to resemble a hospital ward, but as I approached it became apparent the occupants of these beds weren't ill. These were my classmates!

Each of the faces was familiar, all looking like they were blissfully asleep.

However, upon further inspection I realised they weren't asleep at all; they were in some sort of coma. Tubes and wires attached to each body pumped a variety of coloured liquids in and machines monitored each individual bed, but for what I wasn't sure.

As I tried to get a closer look, I heard footsteps outside the door and I rapidly looked around for somewhere, anywhere to hide. Noting a screen at the back, I took my chances and positioned myself so I could see through the slip of a gap.

The two figures from earlier returned, both male but I still couldn't quite make out their faces. They approached a bed and I could hear one say, "The defect must be somewhere in the facility; no bother, it won't get far,"

"They want it retrieved so we'll have to activate one to deal with it," the other replied as he pulled a syringe from his pocket and started injecting it into one of the tubes attached to the figure still lying on the bed.

Activate one? What on earth did that mean? Whatever it was I didn't like it and I wouldn't be hanging around to find out.

As my brain tried to decipher what was going on, I found my eyes being drawn back to the bed and the movement taking place. The figure, a girl no older than myself, sat upright almost robotic in the bed before swinging her legs around and standing to attention.

One of the gentlemen spoke to her, "Agent 618, you have been activated. We have a rogue agent loose in the facility that has become… faulty. We need you to track and return it, intact if possible. Do you accept the parameters of your assignment?"

She looked at him and, in a voice that sent cold shivers down my spine replied, "Understood, verified commencement of assignment." She then exited the room as cool as cucumber with the two figures following her. She was like an empty vessel, devoid of all emotion or human traits. I wondered who the 'rogue agent' could be but it was none of my concern. I needed out of here and the timing was perfect while they were distracted and I could sneak out.

I waited a few moments then took my opportunity, through the door with a glance each way and then off. A chill raced down me and I glanced behind me to see the girl standing there, eyes locked on me, yet it felt like she was looking straight through me at the same time.

Two words came from her, "Target found."

I didn't have to think twice; I ran as fast as I could. Sliding down corridors, still barefoot and feeling the stinging burns against my feet as I skidded round corners.

I didn't dare glance back. I just kept looking forward, and kept running.

If I had looked back I would have realised she was right behind me, I would have realised her arm was about to loop around my throat and I would have been able to duck, but I didn't. Instead, I felt myself falling in slow motion. I felt the crack of my head against the hard floor and I saw her hovering over me with that blank expression, followed by the world falling into darkness.

Twelve: Mairi

I shot up ready to fight. Bram swerved almost losing control of the car, shouting, "Woah! Mairi what'cha doing? Calm down there's no fire!"

Bram. The car. We were still driving. My head was spinning, confused; what on earth was going on? What was actually real? Bram had pulled over on the side of the road and was now looking at me with concern.

"That must have been one heck of a dream. You were mumbling non-stop before you woke up ready to fight the world, are you ok?"

Dream? But I didn't dream. I hadn't dreamt in years, not since… well not since I first went to the Institute, not one single dream or nightmare in fact. Could it have been a dream? Or maybe this was the dream. I didn't know what to think and Bram was still sitting silently staring at me.

"I'm fine, it's just been a long day," I said as I tried to relax. "Sorry for startling you. Let's get moving – we don't want to stay still, we'll attract attention." He looked at me warily but didn't say whatever it was he was thinking.

He turned the engine on and shifted into gear, resuming our journey. Both of us were silent and pensive. I wouldn't be going back to sleep anytime soon, if I was even awake in the first place.

I thought back to the dream and how they referred to the girl not by a name but by a number. What was it? It began with a *6-something*. I tried to think back, 618. Why did that number seem so important, so familiar? I subconsciously twiddled my thumb over my wrist. My eyes glanced down, and then I realised why it was familiar.

619. My thumb ran over my wrist again; over the three numbers etched into my skin. She was 618 and I was 619. I was the defect!

A swarm of thoughts and questions raced through my mind as the car continued its journey. And then I realised it wasn't a dream at all; it was a memory! A memory I had only fragments of up until now. I still didn't have the full picture but now I had a number; *my number*.

The road seemed never-ending, with no turns or distinctive landmarks that I could see. Maybe I was still dreaming? Maybe I had never left the Institute and this was all some sort of sick twisted game. I looked across at Bram who was still silent, looking deep in thought.

Silence, usually peace to my ears, was becoming increasingly more awkward and I shifted uncomfortably in my seat debating whether to talk. As I was just about to open my mouth, I noticed something in the rear-view mirror, approaching fast.

Two blinding lights appeared from behind us, Bram noticed them too as he said, "I get the feeling we have company, hold on tight, this may not be a smooth ride."

He began shifting gears and picking up speed, trying to get some distance between us and them. The car was still drawing closer and as I turned my head to get a better view I could see it coming into focus. I had a feeling they weren't intending to stop.

"Bram, move faster, they're gaining!" I shouted.

"What do you think I'm doing? Going for a leisurely stroll? This car isn't exactly built for speed!" he grunted through gritted teeth as he tried to urge the old car on faster, but it just wasn't going to happen.

We both jolted forward as they rammed into the car; their way of saying Hello. Bram kept a firm grip on the wheel as he kept us steady. Swerving around us, it pulled up side by side with us. I glanced at the dark vehicle but the windows were blacked-out and I couldn't see the driver or if there were any passengers.

Without warning the car veered across the road, swerving

into the front side of our car. Once again Bram attempted to keep control as we zigzagged across the road slightly but managed to stay on, but it wasn't long before they came at us again and… CRASH!

There was no saving us this time. The piercing scream had left my throat before I had a chance to comprehend what was going on. The steering wheel spun out of Bram's grip and a matching look of worry descended across the pair of us as we tried to brace ourselves for impact. Nothing could have prepared us for the chaos that we descended into.

Thirteen: Mairi

I couldn't tell how long we were moving or how many times the car flipped before sliding to a stop on the embankment, but I did know that I had never been more thankful for my seat belt.

Dizzy and feeling the warm trickles of what I assumed to be blood escaping from my head, I yanked myself free from my belt and glanced over to Bram. He wasn't moving and I couldn't see him breathing. Scrambling across I checked his pulse. Thank whatever gods were listening, I hadn't lost him. What I meant was, he wasn't dead. I dragged myself unsteadily round to his side, wrenching the door open and pulling him free of the car. He stirred, groaning as I dumped him down.

My head shot up, I could see lights and hear voices. They were coming to make sure their job was done and there was no way I could get both of us away. Fear started to edge in; I had no choice.

The footsteps kept getting closer and, fear taking over, I whispered to Bram, "I'm sorry." Survival was a cruel game. I climbed a nearby tree to wait for them to leave, breathing as quietly as I couldn't so as not to give my location away.

They found him, still groaning, within seconds. Looking around they realised I was gone. I counted two, no three in total. As one of them kicked Bram in the ribs with a *crack*, I bit my lip forcing myself not to move. I couldn't help him, there was no point both of us being dead.

Another crack from another boot, this time stamping firmly onto his shoulder.

I dug my fingernails into the bark of the tree, feeling the splinters lodge underneath my nails further and further as I dug in deeper. There was nothing I could do now, I should have put him out of his misery before abandoning him but I knew I couldn't have brought myself to do it. Closing my eyes, I tried to block out the sounds of their laughter as they stood over him, watching him writhe in pain as they laughed. No remorse and no guilt, just the pleasure of what they were inflicting on him. A shiver ran across my skin; I knew what would happen next. She was coming out to play. Better late than never.

The change was almost instant, as always. I felt relief as I began to fade, willingly disappearing into the background as the fear shrank within me. It was still me, but not the real me.

I remembered it all, I saw it all like watching a film. It was me, but deep down I knew it wasn't me. She was a warrior from another time, she didn't hesitate or falter and she wasn't confined by my emotions, fears or guilt.

My eyes became sharper, my resolve hardened and any doubts that were there only seconds ago dissipated. With my softer self safely away, my brain began calculating all the viable options and possible scenarios. Like a computer processing data, my brain was hardwired to analyse strategies, percentages and probability. But the speed at which it did so, to the outside eye seemed as though it was action without contemplation.

I dropped from the tree landing with feline grace. I straightened up, a smile creeping onto my lips as their attention rose away from their prey and towards their new toy, ready to play cat and mouse. Only they didn't realise I wasn't the mouse.

Bram was forgotten about and all attention was focused on me as they circled, smug in their delusions of success. The smirks soon vanished as they realised their mistake. As the blade glided effortlessly through the air like a paintbrush, the first two descended towards me. I could see the whole situation play out in slow steps as the world continued on in real-time.

The closest one swung for me, lunging forward. I dropped down, plunging my blade into his foot and causing him to stop. As

I twisted the blade to retrieve it, I could feel the bones grinding as I heard him scream out in pain and he dropped to the floor.

The second one tried to grab me before I elbowed him hard, sending him backwards and giving me room to adjust. As he came back in to try again, he impaled himself firmly on the blade. I pulled the knife across his torso as I imagined it just like gutting a fish. It reminded me of home, the smell of dinner and everything I'd lost. I blinked, it was no time to lose myself.

I looked around for number three, but he was nowhere to be seen. The coward must have fled, so I rounded back on my first friend who was still clutching his foot. Too preoccupied with his pain, he didn't notice me approaching from the rear.

My fingers ran through his hair before yanking back his head. He froze as his fear started catching up with him. My blade softly played against his skin like a bow delicately dancing across a violin, creating a music of its own. He spluttered, grasping desperately at his neck before slumping.

Wiping the blade across the wet grass to cleanse its stains, my mind began to calm and my hands began to shake as I tried to take back control; but she wasn't quite done yet. Just as I was about to stand, I heard a warning cry from Bram. As I turned, I realised it was too late as the shot had already left the barrel.

I wasn't avoiding this one. But I could still protect Bram.

As the bullet impacted against my chest I felt her, the other me, make one last push from deep within as she sent the blade flying towards our missing friend number three. I wouldn't be needing it any longer.

He obviously wasn't expecting it, which was clear from the look of shock as the knife acquainted itself with the main artery of his neck. A great work of art was created as the fountain of red poured from his body and he crashed to the floor.

I smiled as I raised my hands to my chest. My body was catching up with me, as the blood leached out of the wound. Surprisingly, my body was quite numb to the whole situation but as my legs gave out she was already gone and I was left feeling truly alone for the first time.

As the coldness crept over my body and the world blurred, I started to hallucinate shadows running towards me. Hands holding me. The darkness engulfed me and my last thought, as I fearfully slipped from this world with a weak smile, was I didn't have to run anymore.

Fourteen: Mairi

I blinked, shaking myself from my daydream; what a weird daze it was. Straightening myself up, I readjusted in my seat and began looking around the classroom.

As my eyes scanned the room, a few things grabbed my attention. The first was that all the students in the room were not wearing school uniforms. Everyone, myself included, was dressed in matching black attire and boots that reminded me of soldiers you would see in the movies.

The second thing was the silence. None of my classmates were talking, moving or even blinking. Each sat impeccably upright and still, with matching blank expressions; all facing forward, all waiting. But for what?

I stayed silent, looking robotic in order to blend in. A moment later, the Professor walked in. His face was familiar but completely forgettable at the same time. I wondered if I was coming down with something, or maybe I just hadn't read the notice board properly for today's class.

He didn't address the class and hadn't started teaching the lesson, instead he simply sat writing on his clipboard and waiting just like the others. He looked up and three numbers were all that came from him, "553."

A figure rose from their desk and proceeded to the front of the classroom with military precision in every step. The Professor barely acknowledged their presence before saying, "553, your assignment for today will commence shortly; failure will not be acceptable. Do you understand your parameters?"

The boy, whose face I recognized, replied, "Assignment accepted." His voice didn't sound right at all. I tried not to fidget around too much. I still didn't have a clue what was going on but the strange twisting in my stomach suggested it wasn't going to be good. The door opened and two well-built gentlemen dragged a figure in, a bag covering its head.

The figure didn't seem to be able to stand well and when the bag was pulled off he squinted, his eyes trying to adjust to the light. He immediately started stammering, "Please, not this. I'll do better I promise, just give me another chance; I won't let you down again."

His pleas were ignored and as he started to tremble I noticed a trickle of fluid pooling up around his ankle. What would cause a grown man to wet himself in front of a room full of students? I couldn't add up the pieces. What had happened to the history lesson I'm sure was on my timetable?

Trying to ignore the poor man I listened to the Professor speak again, "553, assignment active."

Without further discussion, the student walked up to the man who was now crying and pleading to no one in particular. He walked up behind him with one swift move, so fluid I couldn't keep up with it, before I heard a crack and the man dropped to the floor.

An involuntary gasp slipped from my lips. They killed him! Right there in cold blood, for no reason. Shock gripped my body and I sat there trapped in my own fear, desperately trying to comprehend, as the poor dead man was dragged from the room and the student returned to his seat like nothing had happened. The room began spinning and before I realised it the Professor was speaking again.

In the distance, I could hear him calling another number, "619." That number felt familiar and as I thought about it my body rose from its seat without warning. All control over my body was lost, I was a back-seat driver looking out through the windows of my eyes. I made my way robotically to the front, towards the Professor and the small puddle that remained where the man had previously stood. Just as the last student had, I stood there waiting.

I tried to run, to shout. But it was as though I was shouting from the bottom of a well. Trapped inside my own mind and unable to control myself.

The Professor faced me and said, "619, your assignment for today will commence shortly; failure will not be acceptable. Do you understand your parameters?"

I heard a voice that didn't belong to me escape from my lips, "Assignment accepted." No, No, No. I saw what happened last time; that wouldn't, no, couldn't be me.

But my body just wasn't responding. What was happening to me? I wanted to scream, to cry, to run but no matter how hard I tried my body just wouldn't respond.

A figure was brought in, more petite than the man. The hood was lifted and a young woman was face to face with me. She didn't plea, or shout and cry like the man. No, she simply stood facing me without struggling. A single tear escaped down her face and as she looked at me with a sad smile before she simply said, "I know it's not your fault."

Her face was warm and soft, she had a gentle glow about her even as I heard those three words from the Professor, "619, assignment active."

I couldn't pull my eyes from her. My body began to move towards her and I screamed to stop but no sound came out. It was as though she could see the inner me struggling to get out and she spoke again as the tears rolled freely down both cheeks now, "It's ok, I understand."

I didn't understand what she meant but as I saw my hands raise towards her, dread filled my body. My hands twisted effortlessly and I heard the distinct crack. As her body slumped forwards I instinctively reached out to grab her as the haze lifted from around me.

I heard the words come out of my mouth as the tears began to descend my cheeks, just as hers had stopped. My body quivered as I regained control and cried, "What have I done?"

The Professor and two men all snapped their heads round to look at me as I fell to my knees, cradling the lifeless form; whispering sorry, asking for forgiveness. They stared at me like I had risen from the dead. I could hear them talking in muffled tones.

"That isn't supposed to happen, is it?" asked one of the men.

"No, it's never happened before," the Professor replied, confusion clear in his tone.

"What should we do?" the other man asked.

"Take her down to the labs; they'll know what to do," the Professor instructed.

I felt a shadow over me as my world crashed. I looked up and the Professor was standing over me, holding something in his hand.

"Sssshhhh, just relax, we will fix everything." His words held no reassurance or comfort.

A sharp jab in my neck and the world began to feel distant again, as I felt myself being lifted into the arms of someone strong. The lights dipped in and out as he walked, slowly fading as my eyes grew heavy and the world went black.

Fifteen: Morgan

As Morgan arrived at the secondary location things were underway, teams had begun securing the site and setting up an emergency base of operations. Her superiors had been notified and reinforcements were on their way to help.

A lot of questions required answers. How on earth had anyone found them? It was meant to be a black site with no written records. There must have been a mole within the base, but who? She would have to review everything but for the moment there were more pressing matters ahead.

The list of casualties was extensive. A chill ran down her back as she walked past the bodies lined up in the corridors on trolleys, respectfully covered with simple white sheets; the obituary pages would be full this week. Thankfully she wasn't responsible for the cover-up stories, that was left to her superiors. But it would mean an extensive recruitment drive and now she was even more paranoid about who was around her.

Aileana… She hadn't seen her since the code alert, she should have evacuated in the same transport as her but she couldn't find her anywhere. She had probably stayed behind to ensure all data was destroyed. Morgan's stomach dropped, what if…? No, she couldn't think that way, she was probably here already. Morgan grabbed the nearest person to her that she recognised, a young man called Ferg.

"Ferg, have you seen Aileana? I can't find her anywhere and I need her to help me start setting up."

His eyes shifted, trying not to meet her gaze as he replied, "No ma'am, she is unaccounted for along with Cora, Bram and Mairi.

All other personnel are either here or their bodies have been accounted for. We have a team on route back to the base to search for them now the site has been deemed clear."

Morgan began to shake, bile rising in her throat as she tried to contain herself. Three names she hadn't wanted to hear. But the fourth, Cora, that was one she didn't know. The name sounded familiar for some reason but she couldn't quite place it.

"Ferg, get me all the information you can on Cora immediately." Morgan hoped she was wrong, but if she wasn't and Cora was still alive then she would very quickly wish she wasn't. The only thing to be done now would be to wait for news; she hated waiting, the not knowing, the worrying. Aileana was a smart girl, she'd been with her for years. Morgan didn't have friends or family, but Aileana might as well have been.

Swallowing an uncomfortable lump in her throat, Morgan took a breath. Bram would have gotten Mairi out and if first impressions were to go by the two of them would be able to look after themselves. She had been on the run this long, she highly doubted Mairi would be giving in anytime soon.

As she entered the makeshift office, she picked up the telephone and perched herself on the edge of the old battered desk. Dialling, she waited as the ringing echoed in her ear before a dull voice answered, "Yes?"

"We have arrived at the secondary location; number of casualties being counted as we speak," Morgan quickly relayed. "Four unaccounted for so far. Aileana Heron, my assistant who probably stayed behind to initiate protocols is still missing but teams have gone back to search for her. Bram and Mairi are probably on the move, I want teams out looking for them as a priority as Mairi is vital to mission. Finally Cora, last name I don't currently have, who nobody seems to know much about; I'm waiting for her file to be sent over."

After a short pause the voice on the other end replied, "We will look into the fourth immediately, as for the others, we have had reports from police channels of an RTA and disturbance near the base. I have a team en route to check it out and will update you if it's relevant to your operatives. You've obviously stepped on someone's toes a little too closely for this kind of attack. Keep pressing forward, we need to know who's behind this. We will not tolerate this. All our resources are at your disposal."

The line went dead and Morgan sat contemplating the conversation; oh so *now* they wanted to throw more resources at her. Sighing, she placed the phone back down and turned to sit at her desk with her head in her hands, the weight of the world pressing down as her head throbbed.

She sat, unsure of what to do next but wasn't left to ponder on her own for long. Ferg came rushing back in, out of breath and looking like he had run a marathon.

"Morgan, I mean ma'am. Two personnel en route with a team have been recovered from a crash site. I have no more details but they're about five minutes out, teams are waiting and prepared for all eventualities. We have confirmed one male and one female."

Morgan's heart leapt and sank at the same time, she wasn't sure how much more she could cope with today. If they were two of hers, which two? And were they even alive? She jumped out of her seat, ushering Ferg to lead the way.

Her brain whirled with a million and one thoughts as she briskly strode forward, keeping up with the long strides of the tall blonde ahead of her; unfamiliar with the layout of this base, she hadn't got a clue where they were going. They stopped at a roller door where a team awaited them, consisting of medics and various others. The door creaked and began to rise, giving sight of a loading bay.

The rumble of vehicles could be heard approaching, and as she squinted she could see several dark cars accompanied by a black box van coming quickly into view. Her heart continued to race as every possible scenario played through her mind.

Moments later, she heard the beeping of the van as it reversed up to the bay doors. Morgan held her breath in anticipation.

The doors swung open and out hopped a battered-looking Bram, followed by a stretcher with a female who was not moving. She craned her neck so she could make out the tiny frame… Mairi! She couldn't tell if she was alive or not and it meant Aileana was still unaccounted for, which caused a stabbing in her chest as she thought the worst once more.

Teams flooded around the two, rushing them into the base as the driver stood looking around for who to report to. Torn between following Bram and Mairi and doing her duty, she composed herself before beckoning the driver over. The cool exterior in place, she addressed him, "Report?"

"Yes ma'am," the driver said with a salute, "we had reports of an RTA and disturbance so we intercepted the police and arrived before they could. On arrival, we found five persons; three deceased, not ours. Your agent was barely conscious and we found a young female who we believed to be dead, but your agent had managed to stem the bleeding enough to buy her some time. She is critical and we have no idea of her chances but she's still with us, just barely now." He stood regimental, awaiting further instructions; a soldier through and through.

"Did you find any other females? One petite blonde and the other, I can't quite remember, dark hair I think and quite average looking. I've still got two unaccounted for that we need to find," Morgan asked desperately.

"No ma'am, only the five we encountered. We have brought the bodies back if you wish to view them and the site is currently being cleared."

Morgan felt numb, her only hope now was that Aileana was still at the base. She held tight to the hope as she clenched her hands and said, "No thank you corporal, that will be all. Have your team report in for debriefing, I'll get someone down to look after you."

"Thank you, ma'am."

Morgan was strict but she knew as well as anyone how hard their work was. She always ensured her teams were looked after, part of the reason she inspired such loyalty. She beckoned Ferg over.

"Ferg I'm reassigning you temporarily, you will be taking Aileana's role until we can locate her…" she paused momentarily. "Can you go and help debrief the teams? Make sure they're looked after and report back to me immediately."

A slightly stunned Ferg gaped for a moment before replying, "Yes, ma'am, I'll get straight on it." Aileana's job was one of the most important, it wasn't just given to anyone; not even temporarily.

"And Ferg, close your mouth. You look like a fish like that," said Morgan with a wry smile. Blushing, he nodded and quickly made his exit.

Morgan raced down the corridors trying to remember her way back. Asking for directions once, she found Bram bandaged but sitting upright.

"What happened?" The strain showed in her voice.

"We evacuated, as protocol," Bram replied, wincing in pain periodically. "We were ambushed on the road. They ran us off the road and attacked. Mairi could have got away… but she came back. She saved me. They are working on her now but they don't know if she'll pull through, she's lost a lot of blood. She still managed to kill one as she was bleeding out; you should have seen her!" He coughed, holding his ribs as his body shook. Morgan looked at him, he looked like hell but she needed answers.

"Did you see Aileana? We can't find her and she is completely unaccounted for. I'd hoped she was with you." The look said all she needed to know, like a sharp blow to the gut as Morgan steadied herself against the wall.

"She didn't stand a chance, Cora led her straight into them we think; she was our leak."

Cora, she knew it! Her guts turned at the thought. "And where is Cora?" she asked through gritted teeth.

"She took her own life before I had the chance to do it for her. She told us before she did, though, that she had no choice; they were threatening her family. She looked genuinely scared, so I think she was just a tool."

Morgan swallowed, pushing the sick back down as she thought of her poor Aileana. She didn't ask for any more details as she didn't think she could bear to hear them. She turned to Bram in a daze. And said, "You get some rest Bram; I'll check in with you later. I'm going to check on Mairi's condition."

Slowly turning, she walked out of the room. Her whole world was crashing down around her and there was still so much more to do.

Sixteen: Mairi

A wave of pain like I'd never felt hit me from every angle. I tried to move but the searing pain in my chest was having other ideas. I surveyed my current surroundings. It seemed like I was in a hospital but that was extremely unlikely. So, where was I?

As I pondered my options, a familiar redhead entered the room; apparently surprised to see me awake. Morgan sat down beside me and quietly said, "You're awake, can't keep you down can they? How are you feeling?"

"Alive, surprisingly."

Morgan chuckled, "Yes, we had noticed that. You're definitely resilient, I'll give you that but I think luck may have played a large part this time." She placed her hand gently on mine before continuing, "It was touch and go for a while; you lost a lot of blood. But Bram managed to keep you with us until we could get you fixed."

My mind shifted back, trying to remember what had happened. My alter ego had intervened to save Bram but hadn't managed to save herself. I could vaguely remember feeling the bullet pierce my chest, just as my blade met its target. Everything after that had become a blur, until I had woken up in the classroom. Or at least I thought I had woken up in a classroom. Yet here I was strapped up, with the bullet wound to match. So, I couldn't have been in the classroom. Or maybe I had been previously. The more I thought about it though, the more it occurred to me that these must be memories. But where had these memories come from?

Morgan sat watching me, I couldn't quite read her expression. Those awkward silences used to be peace to my ears, yet around her silence was just uncomfortable. Thankfully, she broke the silence first.

"I'd like to thank you," her voice trailed off softly.

I hadn't got a clue what she was going on about. "Thank me for what?"

She smiled, "For saving Bram of course, you could have left him and saved yourself. You have no real reason to trust us and yet you risked yourself protecting him. For that I thank you, he will be forever grateful. And so will I."

If I thought the silence was awkward before, it was nothing to how I was feeling after her words. I didn't know how to respond, I didn't tell her that I nearly left him. She spoke up again.

"I had a daughter…" She paused as my head shot up, my interest piqued she continued, "I often imagine what she'd be like now, I hope she'd be as brave as you." She broke eye contact, shifting about uncomfortably.

In our brief encounters, Morgan had never betrayed any leaks of emotion or personal details, yet here she was sharing a piece of herself that was obviously still very raw for her. I didn't want to pry but before I could stop myself my big gob was moving.

"Where is she?" Subtlety wasn't a strong point for me.

Morgan's eyes met mine again and a sad smile emerged as she said, "I don't know. She was taken from me a very long time ago and I've been searching for her ever since." Determination lingered in her voice.

"Mairi, I have had numerous reasons for finding you and wanting to help you. Finding my Isla is one of those reasons."

I knew it! Everyone always had a motivation or drive for anything they did, hers was her daughter. Yet even though she had admitted an alternative agenda, I didn't feel betrayed and I wasn't sure why.

"The people that are after you. They weren't always what they are now," she said with a great sadness behind her eyes. "They started off on a very innocent path to try and help people, to make people better. But greed and power took over and they became what they are now. I used to be one of them."

There it was, the revelation I was waiting for; so that's how she knew so much. I didn't betray any expressions or make a sound. I needed to know, I needed the truth so I simply nodded for her to continue.

"I worked at what you know as the Institute. A naïve young scientist, I wanted to make the world a better place. We were working on eradicating disease and weaknesses in human physiology. Volunteers would give birth to children who were genetically enhanced in the embryo stages and we would monitor and nurture the children to see how effective the treatments had been. Or at least that was how it was supposed to be." Morgan stood, uneasily clasping her hands together as she paced back and forth before continuing, "It wasn't until several years in that I found how far from our mission we had strayed. I overheard a meeting between the Professor and several 'businessmen'; he was selling the children! Selling them as assassins, products to be trained and moulded to kill! I knew then and there I had to leave but I was too late. He knew I'd overheard and he had already got to Isla before me."

Morgan's breathing became slightly laboured as she relived the memories she had held onto so tightly for so many years. "He wouldn't give her to me, he said she belonged to him and that I would never see her again if I left. I pleaded and begged but I quickly realised that I wouldn't be able to save her there and then. That was the last time I saw my daughter." She gave a quick sniffle and wiped her eyes. It was clear she was holding back more tears as she continued, "I've been trying to track them and find her ever since. Over a decade of my life, consumed with one purpose. And to be honest I was starting to lose hope, until I heard rumours that someone had escaped the Institute. You. And if you escaped, that means you can lead me back to it. You can help me destroy it and find my daughter."

"Oh," was all I could muster. Not asking for much then. Just wanting me to willingly return to the place I had been running from for so many years. Could I even face those demons?

"Morgan, I'm really sorry but I couldn't help you even if I wanted to. I don't even remember how I escaped, so I have no way of leading you back there."

Seventeen: Morgan

Morgan had been waiting a long time for this moment; she couldn't fail now. Mairi was still a child, yes, she knew that but so was her poor Isla who had endured God knows what. What Mairi failed to see yet was that she would never be free to have a normal life until this ended. Until he was ended. But she would make her see – It was the only way.

She hadn't had the courage to do it all those years ago but she would not make that mistake twice. That decision had cost her everything.

What Morgan had not told Mairi, was that the matter was more complicated than she had divulged. Isla wasn't just her daughter, she was HIS too. Young and naïve she had believed he loved her, that he cared for her and Isla; they were a family. The thought just made her sick now; how she could have ever been that stupid?

Morgan had realised in those months after losing Isla that she had been nothing more than another pawn, that she had been played so perfectly. For weeks after, she desperately searched for them but when she eventually found what she thought to be the Institute it was abandoned and destroyed with no trace of them anywhere. She had never questioned at the time why none of them knew the location. It was all for the protection of the children from activists who wouldn't understand the necessary work they were doing for humanity. Morgan laughed to herself at her stupidity. No, you're an idiot she told herself, it was so nobody could ever lead any unwanted visitors back there.

But now she had Mairi who could lead her straight to him and he would tell her where her daughter was, one way or another.

Morgan glanced across to Mairi, who was now peacefully dozing again. The poor child had already been through so much. The acts she had been forced to commit would haunt her for a lifetime but there was just one more mission, then she could start afresh.

She couldn't give her back her childhood, no, that had been destroyed. But she could at least give her a shot at a second chance of freedom and a life of her own choosing. Mairi was healing quicker than Morgan expected; that wound would have killed any normal person. But that was just it, Mairi wasn't normal.

She slowly exited the room as she pondered the strategies for their next move. This was a game she wouldn't lose.

Eighteen: Mairi

A restless sleep, but no more memories had come to me and the conversation with Morgan was still buzzing round my head. So, I was a chess piece, just another pawn in a game between two sides. The Institute wanted me back. I was a danger to everything they created and Morgan believed I was the key to getting her daughter back and bringing down the Institute as revenge.

I didn't want to play any games; I didn't want to help anyone. I was just tired of running and looking over my shoulder. I needed to end this, one way or another. Sick of being confined to a bed, I spied some clothes nearby that Bram had left earlier.

He had been quite distant since our near-death experience and I got the feeling he was harbouring some guilt about my injuries. Wearily pulling myself out of bed, I donned the clothes, casual but comfy, and stretched. My arms and legs had become weak from lack of use.

I needed some air to clear my head, the four walls of the room were closing in on me and my chest constricted as I looked around. Slowly and stiffly I made my way out into the corridor, a similar layout to the substation base but less modern. People bustled about, not smiling like before but looking more wary; obviously mourning the losses from the betrayal they had faced.

No one paid any attention to me as I wandered the halls and encountered various rooms and people doing curious things. One was a very clean-looking room with a young girl hunched over a workstation, working intently. She glanced up and smiled, signalling me to come in while standing to greet me. "Hi, I'm Evie, you must be Mairi. You're quite the topic around here."

I stood silent, awkwardly unsure of a response. She was very 'quirky' and couldn't seem to stay still, hopping from one foot to the other.

"Everyone's been talking non-stop about how you saved Bram, that was so brave!" she said with a sad smile.

"So, what you working on?" I enquired, swiftly changing the topic to something more neutral. She looked way too excited, obviously desperate to share with someone, anyone. Why had I opened my mouth?

"Something relevant to you actually if you'd like to see?" My interest perked up slightly, I nodded and followed her to her workstation.

She excitedly lifted something small into the light, it looked familiar. My mind flashed back to the bed and breakfast. Standing in front of the mirror, Bram behind me, his breath on my skin, holding my blade and digging it from my flesh.

"My chip?"

She nodded energetically and said, "Well, not your actual chip; we pulled this out of one of the gentlemen you, err, dispatched." My stomach twisted slightly. Pausing briefly, she stared at me before resuming excitedly, "This is like the one you would have had. I've worked out they cannot pinpoint an exact location as the tech they were using was too simple, but they are like a homing beacon sending out a general rough location, hence why they always knew roughly where you were no matter how fast you ran. I've been studying it to see what we can learn."

I had always wondered how they kept up with me so easily. I cautiously asked, "What's to stop them tracking that one and leading them right here?"

She smiled, anticipating the question. "We have taken precautions and the building is protected to block the signal, enabling me to investigate it. I've actually managed to tweak it so it's more accurate." Smiling proudly as she held the small device in front of me.

I looked at the tiny chip, how could something so small have led so much bloodshed to my feet? I tried not to think about it, pushing any flashes back down into the vault. Evie paused to take a call and then excused herself, bouncing out the door with an innocence I couldn't ever recall having. Slightly jealous, I stared at the chip, pondering how different my life could have been. I headed out the door, my head spinning with thoughts and questions.

Nineteen: Bram

Bram entered the room quietly, not wanting to disturb her in case she was asleep. He wasn't sure if he was ready to face her yet but he knew he had to at some point. The room was eerily quiet and as he approached the bed, he realised why. Mairi wasn't in it. Morgan had said Mairi was healing fast but he couldn't quite grasp how fast that seemed to be. She must have been going stir-crazy in here and gone for a walk.

He left the room in search of her, knowing she was probably overdoing it already. The girl didn't seem to know the meaning of slowing down. He searched various rooms but nobody had seen her. She had to be about somewhere, the place wasn't that big. As his mind wandered, thinking about the last few days, he felt a small figure crash into him. He turned to see the culprit and found a very red Evie planted quite awkwardly on the floor.

"Sorry Bram, having a bit of a meltdown. I seem to have misplaced something important. Need to find it before Morgan finds out." She was out of breath and rambling at speed. Bram helped her to her feet trying to calm her.

"Evie," he sighed, "you're the most thorough person I know; you never lose anything. Talk me through where you had whatever it was and we'll retrace your steps." He hoped he would casually bump into Mairi on the way too so the pair headed back to Evie's lab and began to retrace her steps together.

"I was working on the precision tracking on the chip we pulled out of one of the deceased gentlemen you and Mairi encountered. I was just calibrating the chip when Mairi popped by. I was chatting away with her about my work and then I had a call."

She positioned herself where she had been and Bram watched her re-create her movements. So, Mairi was around then; he could catch her after he helped Evie. Evie was always a worrier and got stressed very easily but was by far the most advanced in her field. He continued to watch as she spoke again.

"I couldn't get a good signal, due to the signal blocking, so I left the room to take the call and when I returned I couldn't find it. I thought I must have knocked it on the floor when I rushed out but I can't find it anywhere. I was going to see if Mairi would help me look but by the time I'd got back she'd already gone. I figured she must have a lot on, she seemed quite distracted."

Bram clicked. "So, you didn't see Mairi leave?"

Evie shook her head, looking confused.

"And you told Mairi exactly what you'd been doing, here with the chip?"

Evie nodded enthusiastically as she replied, "But don't worry, I reassured her that they couldn't track the chip here inside the building as the signal was being blocked. You'd need to be well off the premises before the chip signal could register." She smiled, confident that she had reassured Mairi she was safe inside the compound. Bram didn't seem to share her smile though.

"Did I do something wrong? Bram, did I say the wrong thing?"

"No, Evie you didn't do anything wrong, but I must go," Bram said reassuringly as he moved towards the door. "I have some errands to catch up with, you know Morgan will be on my case if I don't get it done." Evie nodded sympathetically; Morgan expected only the best and was never one to be let down, by anyone.

Bram politely excused himself and hastily left the lab, picking up speed as he rounded the corner. No, she wouldn't have, she couldn't have. Why would she?

With a million questions and worry he knew he shouldn't be feeling for his charge, he barged into Morgan's office, breathless and rambling.

Morgan looked startled at his dishevelled state and said, "Bram breathe, then speak; I can't work out a word you're saying." She handed him a glass of water, which he sipped before trying again.

"Mairi's gone, she's left the compound and she's taken a tracking chip with her. They'll be hunting her like an animal, she doesn't realise what she's done."

Morgan looked at the expression on his face, which was more than just simple worry for his charge, but she didn't say anything. Instead, she sat thinking about the revelation before replying in an urgent tone, "Perhaps she thinks she knows exactly what she's done. However, I think she underestimates the gravity of what she's running into. Get me Evie immediately. We can't let her do this alone."

Bram nodded before swiftly exiting the room, leaving Morgan with her thoughts. The child was either incredibly brave or ridiculously stupid. Regardless, she wasn't running anymore; now the hunter, no longer the prey. If this played out right, both could get their second chance. But every step on the board mattered now.

Moments later a confused and panicking Evie entered Morgan's office. "Morgan, I can explain, honestly; I don't know where it's gone but I promise I will find it."

"Shhh will you," Morgan quietened her by raising a hand, she couldn't stand the girl whimpering. For someone so intelligent, she panicked about absolutely everything; it was quite irritating at times. "You won't find it because it isn't there."

Evie's face paled and Bram prepared to move in case she fainted, a likelihood with her sensitive nature. Morgan couldn't cope with mothering the woman, so swiftly put her out of her misery. "Don't worry it's not your fault, however we do need your help to try and track the person who did take it."

Evie's face straightened and she immediately perked up, "I can do that! I tweaked the chip so that we could track it at all times, I just need access to my laptop from my workroom!"

Morgan breathed, well at least that was one piece of good news. They could track Mairi. The question was, what would they walk into when they found her? Strengthening her resolve, she turned to Bram, "Assemble a team, small and specialist; you know who to pick. Evie, get me a location on that chip… now!"

Evie scampered away like a mouse while Bram moved purposefully off to prepare. He wouldn't forgive himself if anything happened to Mairi, he owed her his life and that was a debt he wasn't comfortable with.

Twenty: Mairi

A plan would have probably been a good idea, but I'd never had one before so why start now? Hopefully, I had enough of a head start that they wouldn't be able to catch up with me. No point in everyone else getting killed as well. I just hoped I could hold my nerve; my stomach was already in knots with my hands clamming up as I held them together awkwardly.

I'd run for so long, trying to avoid death, yet here I was walking into an almost certain suicide mission. My only regret was that had I done this sooner, maybe my mother wouldn't have paid for my false hope of freedom.

I sat in a nearby train station watching the people go by, it actually felt quite peaceful. I wondered how it would feel to live as they did, to have their worries and problems instead of my own. A little girl clutched a tatty teddy bear in one hand and held tightly onto a woman's hand with her other. I could feel the glow of warmth as the woman, who I presumed to be her mother, looked fondly down at the child.

I could almost remember the warmth of my mother's arms tightly wrapped around mine, the fuzzy tingle in my stomach as she kissed me and told me she loved me.

My last memories of her were far from warm or fuzzy.

***

Banging on the door to our house, I saw the look of panic as she found me barely able to stand or talk. She dragged me inside, her maternal instincts kicking in. She didn't know what had happened, only that her daughter needed her. Hushing me and telling me to rest I managed two words which swung her into action, "They're coming…"

She obviously didn't know who or what but she jumped straight up, using all the strength in her tiny body to place me delicately in the nearest closet. Kissing me softly and reassuring me everything would be ok, as I struggled to stay conscious. She closed the door as I watched her footsteps through the vent, ensuring all trace of me was hidden.

The knock came too soon. She answered calmly, though I could detect the underlying quiver in her tone; it was slight, but it was there. They didn't dispense with the niceties.

I tried to get up, but every part of my body was drained. My brain was screaming, kicking me to help her as she screamed in agony but still refused to give me up to them. I slipped into the darkness as my body finally gave in.

When I awoke, I wished I hadn't. Crawling from the cupboard and the sanctity of its protection, my hand pressed in something cold and unusual; not water, much darker. Not quite black but thick, dark and slightly red. My eyes followed its path.

My heart shattered as my world ended. All in a split second.

Her contorted body reached out towards me; eyes still open, tortured yet lifeless. Her fingernails, usually beautifully painted and polished, were missing. Raw flesh and blood replacing where they had been mercilessly ripped out, one by one. My mind flashed, remembering the screams as she suffered; protecting me to the very end.

Snapping from my daze I heard footsteps out the front, they were still here; hoping I'd show up no doubt. A whirlwind of emotions attacked me and fought for control as I threw up everything I had in my stomach, shaking and sobbing until a gentle click and wave of calm overcame me

That was the first time she emerged.

I felt myself slipping into the passenger's seat and I immediately felt safe. I didn't know how or why but I knew she would protect me, just as my mother had done to the very end. She gently placed her fingers over my mother's eyelids, softly closing them as she placed a tender kiss on her head; asking for forgiveness, hoping she had found peace.

I felt the new driver of my body stand, not with fear or pain but with purpose, and I knew in that moment every scream my mother had given for me was about to be returned in kind.

***

As I sat relieving the memories of that day and the events that followed, I saw them. They weren't hard to miss; suits neatly pressed, ties perfectly made and a walk that shouted 'we're here'. For the first time ever I took control, putting my warrior away out of sight; it was the mouse's turn to play with the lions.

Twenty-One: Alistair

Alistair's head felt like it was going to explode, with a headache that could have probably levelled a city. He had several impatient clients wanting their products and his own little problem was still niggling at the back of his mind. He knew they would recover it eventually but it needed to be before anything was leaked publicly. And then there was the matter of his unwelcome friends, another unexpected blip. Unsure quite what the full extent of their knowledge was, it was worrying him slightly to say the least. The informant he had managed to place had been about as useful as a goldfish and hadn't found out anything, except for the fact they were looking for it as well. Answers weren't coming easily, but the headaches definitely were.

His thoughts flickered to Morgan, he knew he probably should have killed her at the time. It would have tied up a few loose ends. But something, he couldn't quite work out what, had stopped him. It may have been a mercy he would live to regret but deep down he knew he still had feelings for her. If only she had shared his vision, it wouldn't have been a problem.

He headed down to the meeting room, where his clients sat waiting. Who they were and where they were from was irrelevant, anonymity protected both himself and the clients in all transactions of this nature. The less he knew the better.

Nodding politely, he welcomed the guests, "Welcome, welcome. I'm so honoured by your interest to do business with us. I take it my team have briefed you on the minor details?" The translator between them relayed the greeting enthusiastically and the clients nodded, smiling broadly.

"Well then, let us begin the demonstration; wouldn't want you paying before being satisfied with your purchase." Alistair nodded to the security guard standing next to the door and he opened it. Two figures entered: An academic-looking figure first – one of the scientific team that he couldn't remember the name of – quite twitchy and unable to hold his fingers still as he entered, followed closely by a young girl in her early teens, silent and expressionless. She moved effortlessly into the room, standing centrally for all to see.

The academic looked around the room and began to speak, "Professor, visitors, welcome. I hope your journey has been a comfortable one. I am happy to present to you our latest product and upgraded model: The series 700." Still twiddling his fingers, he gestured to the young girl who was still silent and statuette-like; almost oblivious to her surroundings.

"Faster, stronger and with a higher rate of restoration, this model outstrips the older models by a considerable margin," the academic continued as he circled the young girl. "Unlike our older models, this one is also able to assimilate and interact in public settings without any attention being drawn. Once programmed, personality algorithms and languages can be installed, uploaded and changed as required."

The translator spoke quickly, relaying the information as the visitor's eyes lit up like children at Christmas. Alistair's head was still banging, he was desperate to get back to his office for updates and so he stepped in to speed things along.

"How about we give these gentlemen a demonstration? I'm sure they are eager to complete their transaction and get on their way with their new product."

Again they smiled, nodding eagerly to see their product in action. Another two figures entered: A large, suited gentleman dragging a smaller figure into the room with a bag over their head. The figure was thrown to his knees and the bag was pulled off. His eyes squinted as they readjusted to the light.

"You can't do this to me!" he screamed, "Don't you know who I am? I'll have your jobs for this, I may be a prisoner but I have rights. I'll talk you know!"

Alistair shifted to the edge of his seat and softly spoke, "Mr Ryan, is it? Unfortunately, nobody is going to care about you; a murderer and a thief. Although it is sad that you tragically died whilst trying to escape prison, the prison system is so overstretched that they won't have the time or resources to investigate." Alistair watched with slight enjoyment as the panic began to spread over Mr Ryan's face.

"ESCAPE! What? The hell I did, you abducted me and brought me here; there's no way anyone would believe that story." The conviction of his words didn't quite meet his eyes.

Smiling, Alistair looked at his trembling hands and offered him a glimmer of hope, "Ok then Mr Ryan, you seem like a pretty decent chap; I tell you what, I'll make you a deal. If you can beat this young lady here in a fight, I'll let you go, completely free. No jail, no punishment; just simple freedom. Here, I'll even give you a knife so it's not an unfair fight."

If Mr Ryan had looked confused before it was nothing compared to his expression now, or the bemused looks around the room from the foreign visitors who looked like all they were missing was the popcorn.

"But she's a little girl, she couldn't hurt me, don't you know who I am?"

Picking up a file from the nearest table Alistair opened it and said, "Yes, Mr Ryan, actually I do. Glasgow born and raised. First murder at age 17, your mother's boyfriend. At least thirty-five kills since then, that we know of. Skilled in both martial arts and hand-to-hand combat, you have made your money and reputation over the years as the Highland Killer for hire. Men, women and children; no job ever turned down. Yes, Mr Ryan, we know all about you." He could see the confidence building in Mr Ryan's eyes as he weighed up his options.

Still trying to work out what was going on, he pulled himself to his feet triumphantly and said, "Let's get this over with, I've got things to do."

Alistair nodded to the visitors who seemed to be thoroughly enjoying the narration of the translator, before turning to the academic, whose name he still didn't have a clue about, to begin.

The academic turned to the girl and began to speak, "Agent 702, activate. Task – combat and extermination, do you accept your parameters?"

Without looking at him she nodded, "Task understood and accepted."

Mr Ryan had a glimmer of worry again as he watched the exchange, Alistair loved watching that internal struggle as the man tried to work out if any of it was real. He took the knife offered to him and wasted no time in trying to secure his freedom.

He lunged at the girl, who sidestepped effortlessly. Twisting round, he swiped his arm towards her with the blade extended. Again she dodged cleanly, leaning backwards slightly until his arm was fully extended across her body. She promptly placed her hands at either end of his arm and with one swift move the CRACK was heard throughout the room, followed by the clatter of the knife to the floor. Mr Ryan's dull voice moaned out in shock and pain as he tried to distance himself from her and regain his ground.

She slowly walked towards him as his eyes frantically looked around for a replacement weapon. Eager to make a good show for his visitors, Alistair slid the knife across the floor to him, smiling encouragingly as Ryan grasped at it with his good hand. All technique and ability were gone, replaced by panic and pain as he tried to launch an attack whilst shielding his damaged limb.

He was dead already, he just hadn't accepted it yet. As he tried to land a futile blow he left his guard wide open and she took the invitation without hesitation, delivering an effortless yet powerful blow right to the throat, stopping him in his tracks. He stood, eyes wide as he dropped the knife and grasped at his neck with his good hand, desperate for air that wasn't coming. As he coughed and spluttered, life slipping out of him, he fell to the floor but was gone before his head made contact.

Mission completed, the young girl resumed her original stance; neither phased nor out of breath. Perfection. Alistair Crowland's life's work, so beautifully crafted. As security removed the former Mr Ryan, he stood to address the guests.

"And that completes our demonstration, if you are wholly and fully satisfied with what you've seen I will get one of my team down to finalize the transaction and prepare 702 for transportation. Remember that included in your aftercare package is regular health checks, and software updates can be provided, for an additional fee of course." He respectfully shook the hand of each of his guests as the translator confirmed their delight at the product's capabilities before beckoning a member of security to escort them down to the waiting room. As they headed off, excitedly chatting, O'Reilly – the head of security – came in.

"Professor you're needed. The package has been secured."

Best news he'd had all day! Excusing himself, he dashed quickly back to his office for a full debrief. He wasn't quite sure what to expect, but it certainly wasn't the sight he walked into. Alistair turned to the attendant who had been assessing it and called him away out of earshot.

"Hello Miles," he said with faux affection. Miles nodded enthusiastically, ever the faithful lapdog. He had his uses, so Alistair allowed his delusions that they had some sort of friendship to keep him compliant and loyal. "So, what do we know then?"

Miles glanced across the room thoughtfully before deciding how to proceed. "Well we don't know much at the moment to be honest Professor, all initial tests have come back clear and we can't find any source of corruption to explain the data loss. We should do more tests to see what we can find out. We are just finalising the newest batch to go out for prep and then we will continue testing on the package."

Alistair didn't know whether to be annoyed or relieved; the data loss was concerning as information shouldn't be able to be erased, however the return of the package was more important. Answers could be sought later. Progress couldn't be delayed on the new batch placements.

Twenty-Two: Mairi

Still unsure if this was the smartest or stupidest thing I'd done, I ignored my inner self itching to get out along with every fibre of my being telling me to run. Instead, I followed my escorts out of the lavish car to the building ahead. The imposing structure resembled a stately home and a shiver trampled down my spine as the view retrieved memories of my last visit here, along with my awkward departure.

A beautifully sculpted building on the outside, I now knew the ugliness it held within. I compliantly followed as they spoke softly, trying to reassure me that everything would be ok now I was home and that they would take care of me. How freely those lies spilled from their tongues like venom, dripping out with each word.

Oh, I knew exactly how they wanted to take care of me.

I steadied myself, trying to keep my waning composure by thinking of Bram, of Morgan and my mother. I couldn't let anyone else get hurt for me again. This would stop with me one way or another, I couldn't falter now. Led through a beautiful entrance hall to an enchantingly carved set of doors, I waited, knowing the belly of the beast was not so delicately concealed under its shell.

The doors opened and all sense of the warm homely welcome vanished, instead replaced by cold clinical walls and corridors leading to rooms of horror that flooded my memories. The temperature instantly dropped, as the sickening tingle crept through my body. I could feel the warrior itching to get out again, but I shushed her back down while trying to contain my fear. It wasn't time… yet.

At the fourth door on the left, we stopped. They still kept up the charade of concern and warmth, they could have been quite convincing if I didn't already know better. A man in a white coat stood welcoming me and, showing me to a medical couch, he began to speak.

"Do you know who I am?" he asked softly.

Not trusting my voice, I shook my head meekly; of course I recognized him. My mind flashed back, that poor woman. The flashes I now knew were memories. His words still echoed through my head – *'619, assignment active'*. I could feel the crack of her neck in my hands and the weight of her body slumped against me as I realised what I'd done. I would never forget his face, burned into my mind as I closed my eyes. He smiled at me and continued to speak.

"Do you know where you are?"

I took a breath, thinking carefully; the mouse must play her part. I nodded and in barely above a whisper I said one word, "Home."

"Yes, that's right my dear you're home and we'll make sure you stay nice and safe here with us. I just want to do some tests to make sure you're not… unwell."

I nodded, needing to bide my time. I couldn't waste the right opportunity by acting too soon. He and his colleagues took readings and measurements. They asked questions and took blood, racing around like I was a new puzzle to play with. My friends who had brought me home were still with me, no longer smiling but conveniently placed near the door to ensure I was safe and secure.

It was hard to track time, but after what felt like an eternity the door opened and in he walked. I didn't need to retrieve any memories to know who he was. I didn't even need a name. The stench of all this radiated off him as he strolled into the room and everyone immediately became nervous, including me.

He took the man he referred to as Miles to one side, talking in tones I couldn't quite make out but the topic of their discussion was obvious. I could feel something bubbling under the surface of my skin. Gripping onto what waning control I had, I tried to assess the situation, keeping my meek little mouse playing host with the doctors while the other me assessed the room from the backseat.

Only one entrance in or out. Two trained and almost definitely armed guards obstructing the door. I could probably get out, but what then? I didn't know enough of what lay waiting for me beyond those doors to work the odds out effectively, my only choice was to stay put and hope for an opening.

He glanced over at me and smiled. As he headed towards me, I tried to calculate the best course of action; they had to think I wasn't a threat. In a moment of madness as he approached, I wrapped my arms around him and began hugging him like a small child. He froze, taken aback as I continued to hug him and waited for the next move.

"There, there, child you're home now; don't you worry, I will take care of you."

Another trained liar, as he looked me in the eye reassuringly he might as well have been stabbing me in the front and back at the same time. He held out a hand to me as he said, "Come, let's get you some food and some warm clothes."

I took his hand as softly as I could, hoping the clamminess didn't spark any suspicion as I allowed him to lead me out of the room. The two guards followed, though at a distance this time and looking visibly more relaxed. They would regret that eventually. As we walked I memorized the routes, reminding myself of layouts and locations of value; no point looking at escape routes, as I probably wasn't leaving here alive.

It was almost easy to slip into believing the false cover they gave, with the caring smiles and warm tones I had to keep reminding myself that it didn't exist. It was all fake and this had been my prison. We turned a corridor and as I glanced right a memory fleeted past… The holding areas! That's where the others would be. Storing the location for later I followed him into a room that didn't fit with the coldness of the outside corridors.

There was a warm, roaring fire next to two snug chairs and behind them a grand wooden dining table that mirrored the exterior style of the stately building's theme.

He gestured toward one of the chairs, "Come sit child, rest. I can't imagine what you've been through out there all alone. Let's get some warm food inside you and get you comfortable."

Not once did he use my name, only confirming I was nothing more than a number to him, just as his own child had been before he had stolen her from Morgan all those years past.

"So, you don't remember anything? Nothing at all?"

I shook my head, trying to look as blank and vacant as possible.

"You poor thing, don't worry we'll figure everything out and fix this horrible mess."

Walking to his desk, he scribbled something on a piece of paper before giving it to one of his guards to take away. My window would need to appear soon or my sacrifice may be pointless, I was losing my nerve by the minute; I wasn't like her. I just wanted to go home to my mum and hide in her arms, as impossible as that was. The guard returned with a tray, the smell of warm soup filled my nostrils and I had to admit it smelled good. He sat it down at the table and gestured for me to eat.

I was wary that it could be laced with poison or something worse, but also aware if I didn't eat it they might suspect something was amiss. I had no choice. I raised the spoon slowly to my mouth, aware of the eyes currently studying me. I let the hot soup tease against my lips, as it met my tongue I knew it was too late; I was at their mercy.

I waited, nothing tasted off that I could detect and I didn't feel any different. I continued to eat, hoping it was soup and nothing more. Time would tell.

Twenty-Three: Morgan

Just as Evie had promised, she tracked the location of the chip. Morgan had something she'd never had before: A destination. In all her years of searching, they had never been able to find even a glimmer of it but Mairi had done it. Possibly at her own peril.

The chip couldn't tell if Mairi was alive or not, just her location, so they were going in expecting the worst. The teams were briefed, their mission was to secure the area and extract the children. Morgan however had a mission of her own and her target was more singular. HIM.

She knew he would be in there and she knew he would have the answers she wanted. One way or another she was going to get them. Bram on the other hand was still holding out hope for Mairi's safety, which worried Morgan. He was distracted and that would be dangerous for everyone, but nobody could tell him any differently.

With the entire team gathered she explained, "The children's safety is the priority, remove any threats that come between you and their extraction. By any means necessary."

They all acknowledged with a nod. Splitting into several smaller teams they headed in different directions, just leaving Morgan, Bram and two others behind.

Bram took the lead for tactical arrangements, radioing all groups currently on the move, "Take position around the perimeter, spread yourselves to as many locations as you can. We want to hit them in as many different places as possible and disperse any security that may be lurking. I want a simultaneous assault on my command, do you all understand?"

All teams responded, acknowledging the orders and confirming they were in place. There was no going back. Morgan knew there was a chance her Isla wouldn't be there. Children were usually put out into foster homes until they were of a suitable age then brought back to the Institute for studying, or as she had discovered, 'training.' But she couldn't give up, she was her mother. There was always a hope that he hadn't used her, a glimmer anyway.

Her mind drifted to Mairi as she waited for the teams to get into position. So many unanswered questions; a perfect killing machine trapped inside the body of an innocent girl, how would she eventually face the horrors of what she had endured, if she was even still alive? Morgan shook the thought from her head, Mairi was a resourceful person and she would be fine… she hoped.

The teams all signalled they were in place, with no visible signs of security or threats.

"Don't be fooled. It will be there," Morgan warned, she knew what they were capable of; these were mercenaries not scholars. Hopefully they would have the element of surprise, they could use all the help they could get.

Taking a deep breath, she realised this was what she had spent her life working towards. Since losing Isla, her world had fallen apart. Everything since then had been a journey to this point. To him. To revenge.

"Move in."

The world became hazy as they descended on the building. It was as though time had slowed, but her heart still pounded like a thousand drums calling out to declare war. She wasn't a fighter and hated violence, but she held her gun firmly with an unwavering resolve that had been building for many years. Her team surrounded her as they entered. The sounds of chaos began emitting from all directions. The other teams had breached the building too, and apparently found the security.

The surreal moment bullets started firing towards her, she thought about how much more scared she thought she would be.

Yet as the rain of gunfire exchanged between the two sides, she effortlessly slipped into her role while firing towards oncoming attackers.

It was the first time she'd ever used a gun against a real person. Years of target practice had ill-prepared her for the graphic reality of her bullet making contact with another human being. Ricocheting through its target and crippling the towering figure, it pulled him to his knees as he began grasping at the hole that now leaked from his abdomen. She watched as he keeled over, succumbing to his fate.

The hall silenced but the echoes of gunfire and conflict could be heard in the distance. Bram carefully assessed the damage; two of theirs lost and one injured, a flesh wound which could be sorted later. He strapped up the injured one and turned to Morgan.

"We need to keep moving," he breathed heavily, "there will be more coming soon. The other groups can handle extraction but we need to do what we came for, no distractions"

Morgan looked at him, the usually chilled out persona gone and replaced with The Agent. Cold robotic and mission orientated. He was the best in his field for a reason, too many underestimated him. Loyal to his mission and never distracted, well almost. Morgan was still wary of his attachment to Mairi but she didn't mention it, it wasn't the time. If they survived it could be discussed later.

The team moved cautiously until they came to an occupied room, fourth door down on the right. Security was nowhere in sight but one figure had taken refuge in there. The figure immediately paled as he noticed Morgan enter through the door.

"Hello Miles, long time no see." Morgan watched as he quivered, looking like he'd seen a ghost.

"Morgan! What are you doing here?" Miles trembled, fiddling with his hands and unable to stay still.

"You know exactly why I'm here Miles, now tell me where he is."

"I don't know, he left with her earlier, honestly I don't know where they are," Miles cried while frantically searching for a way out of his current predicament. "Don't do anything you'll regret Morgan, you're a good person and you don't want to do anything silly."

Morgan's body tensed as she rounded in on the man she once called friend, there was no need for words. He pleaded as the shot rang out, silencing his cries. She would pay for her actions later, just as he had just paid for his.

Bram looked at her cautiously, wary of her emotional state, but she stood composed and calm and nodded reassuringly to him.

"Let's keep moving team," Bram snapped as he took control again, "eyes on the doors for movement, I'll take lead. Morgan, you follow me."

She nodded, focused and ready as the team assembled in formation and swiftly moved out, leaving the lifeless corpse of Miles without a second glance. More judgement and retribution were still to be served.

They rounded the corner to find a scattered assortment of bodies littering the floor, Morgan counted six: Four of theirs and two of hers. She felt a twang of guilt, pushing the feeling down as she reminded herself that every cause had its casualties. Bram checked the bodies to confirm none were alive. One of the bodies groaned and he swiftly swung around. Not one of theirs. He moved across to the body, gun in hand, aiming the weapon; one shot to the head and the groaning was no more.

Further down they a door guarded by two security officers, they hadn't noticed them yet. Silently, Bram gestured to a stocky figure to the rear of the group holding a long bag on his back. He nodded and, putting the gun in his hand away, retrieved the long rifle from its slender case.

Crouching down, he focused himself on the two unsuspecting guards at the far end of the corridor. Two consecutive pops emitted from the weapon, followed by the heavy slumps of the men. They hadn't even seen it coming. Probably better that way, unlike Miles who had certainly seen his end.

They approached the door. Flanked by the remainder of the team, Bram surveyed the surroundings. He went to open the door as Morgan peered over his shoulder and he twisted the handle. They prepared themselves for the next round of conflict.

Twenty-Four: Mairi

As I slowly finished the soup, I noticed the two guards had left. I presumed they were still outside though as I surveyed the room. No other obvious exits, apart from the windows and the door we had come through. As I placed the suspicious bowl gently on the table next to me, my companion currently with his back towards me turned and approached.

With a cold smile he said, "We have been so worried about you. You don't realise the trouble we've gone through to find you and ensure you returned to us… safely." His face was blank as he studied mine, there was something tickling at the back of my mind. I couldn't quite put my finger on it but it was almost as if she were shouting to me through a bustling crowd, her voice distant and muffled. I stared into the warm fire, my body basking in the warmth of the open flames. Haze filled my mind and I struggled to focus. There was something I was meant to be doing, I'm sure, but my eyes were so heavy.

I could hear his muffled footsteps approach and a hand gently sweep my hair from my face. Softly his voice came, "Sleep my little one, you're home now and I won't lose you again."

Screaming from the clouded prison she was surrounded in, my focus faded as my brain desperately tried to stay awake clinging to those words – my little one. What did he mean, was it just a turn of phrase? Succumbing to the inviting warmth, I entered its embrace and slipped softly away.

***

As the haze lifted I found myself lying in a bed, darkness surrounding me as I strained my eyes trying to see where I was. Tubes connected to my arms, filled with fluids. I yanked them out sharply, the sting soaring through my arm. Still disorientated as my brain tried to process what was going on, I looked around and instantly knew.

Beds in rows on either side of the room, each with a sleeping occupant, each being pumped with fluids of various colours and looking peaceful in a dream-like state. I could hear movement and in a desperate move I lay back down, placing the wires underneath me and hoping they wouldn't notice. I froze, listening carefully to hear what was going on.

"Have you decided yet what you're going to do with her? She's nearly of age and her training is more than complete now Professor."

"No not yet Miles. Is anyone else aware of who she is?"

"No sir, everyone still thinks she is Mairi. But if we don't look at doing something with her soon, she may start to attract attention. She's older than all the rest. May I ask, is it a personal connection with the girl because she's yours and hers?"

"Mind your place and your tongue Miles. You overstep your boundaries with things that do not concern you." I could hear feet shuffle, I presumed belonging to Miles.

"I'm sorry sir, I didn't mean to offend, I only want to ensure what is best for you and the Institute."

"She is only still here because of the anomaly in training, she should not have had an emotional leakage during it. None have ever awoken during the training. We need to learn why." I could hear the footsteps fade as my mind reeled.

"Yes sir, but it hasn't happened before or since so I honestly just think it was a one-off."

"Well we need to be sure; she stays here until we are"

The door closed and I shot up, my chest pounding and unable to breathe. Their words resounding in my head. I jumped out of the bed disorientated, the floor spinning beneath me as I came crashing to the ground and the blackness engulfed me once more. This was becoming too much of a regular habit.

Twenty-Five: Alistair

As he watched her drift off, Alistair swept a loose piece of hair from her face, mumbling to himself as the soup took effect. He could see just how much she looked like her mother. Shaking himself from the thought and back to the matter at hand, Alistair began to review the situation.

He was relieved to have her back, it was too dangerous for her to be loose; she could have exposed everything. But if he was honest with himself, he was also relieved she was back safely. Not that he would openly admit it but he'd watched her grow from a distance, monitoring her progress while trying not to form an attachment. Yet every time he saw her face, the memories of the three of them would flash back.

They were just dreams now though; the projects had to come first. He'd gone past the point of no return and yet he still hadn't been able to let her go completely. She was still his link to who he was before he had started down this path. Alistair had sold his soul a long time ago and had very few regrets but he had always been curious of the what-ifs.

Alistair knew he needed to decide what to do with her though. He couldn't put her back under, she was too much of a risk to put back now as she'd snapped out of the conditioning twice. And of course, there was the possibility of irreversible neurological damage. Maybe he wasn't as soulless as he tried to convince himself he was, he thought reflectively.

Alistair wasn't convinced she was as blank as she was letting on either, these were dangerous weapons disguised as children that he had created and essentially so was she, he knew he couldn't forget that. The soup had bought him some time to decide how to proceed, he thought perhaps if he spoke to her he could get her to see things logically. She was just as much his as her mother's, she might have his sense. One could hope. He could dare to dream of having a daughter to inherit his life's work.

Shaking himself from the pipe dreams, he knew he needed to stay focused. If she was back it meant they would be looking for her and him. Precautions would have to be put in place to ensure the Institute and its work were safeguarded. Walking over to his desk, Alistair glanced once more at her still sleeping form, she was dreaming about something, slumbering innocently. Picking up the phone he dialled 7.

"O'Reilly, can we assess all locations and local teams immediately? Ensure everything is secure and tighten everything up for now, we must remain vigilant."

"Of course, Professor Crowland, I'll get right on it."

He placed the phone back down with a click, most just called him Professor, it was only ever O'Reilly who ever used his actual name. The last time anyone had called him by his first name was another lifetime ago.

His mind wandered back to her innocent smile.

"Ali, I love you, you do know that don't you?" She could always make him blush.

"Don't call me that in public, others may hear. It's not… appropriate." She'd always follow it with a deviant wink, "Yes ALISTAIR, PROFESSOR SIR!" The cheeky minx.

What he wouldn't have given for things to have turned out differently. Her betrayal had been his biggest shock. Alistair had been convinced she would eventually see that what he was doing was important, he had no choice. He knew the government were never going to support his work properly; they were too scared of real progress. The work had to come first. At any cost.

Alistair clasped at his head, it was clouded and fuzzy which was never productive. He had to be focused. He just couldn't decide what to do for the best, with all this uncertainty he would just have to wait for her to wake and see how things unfolded.

Sitting opposite her he soaked in every detail, noticing with a pang of regret the tiny scars on her arms. He wondered how she'd got them. Reaching out gently, he touched one of her wrists. An unfamiliar tug pulled at his gut. He knew he was responsible for every scar, every bad thing she had experienced. Maybe if she had been pulled out of the training sooner, he thought, none of this would have happened; the joy of hindsight. But the future could be different, he had a glimmer of hope.

Unsure of exactly how long he sat there watching over her, she eventually began to stir with a groan. She sleepily stretched and with a soft yawn her eyes came into focus as she glanced around the room.

"Are you ok? You fell asleep. I didn't want to disturb you as you seemed like you needed it." It wasn't exactly a lie, he just left out the extra ingredients he had put in her soup.

She nodded silently with a meekness that surprised him.

"Mairi, I know you're confused. I know you want answers; I think we need to talk."

Her eyes betrayed her and flickered only for a second but enough to confirm she wasn't as blank as she was portraying, that was ok, she could hide behind her act for now. He thought carefully about how to proceed, twiddling his fingers anxiously before opening his mouth.

"There's so much to tell you Mairi, but I'm not quite sure where to sta—"

CRASH! Two shots came from outside the room. Mairi's head shot up, alert; there was that inbuilt training running in the background. They had company. Before he could say anything further the doors came crashing open and a haunting image of beauty right out of his dreams stood before him.

Morgan stepped over the lifeless corpses that had been guarding the door. Head held high with more confidence than she had, she strutted into the room, weapon poised and instantly trained on its inhabitant.

"Hello, Alistair."

Twenty-Six: Mairi

I could feel the warmth of the fire tickling my face, teasing me back to the world, I was so comfortable though that I didn't want to move. My brain slowly started to come into focus, reviewing and processing everything my flashback had revealed.

Not Mairi?
Professor's child?
World spinning.

Slowly I opened my eyes and noticed the set trained right back at me from across the room.

"Are you ok? You fell asleep? I didn't want to disturb you as you seemed like you needed it."

I had my doubts about the necessity of my sleep, I knew I shouldn't have eaten that soup. But I was still alive, which I suppose was some small consolation. Not trusting myself to speak yet as I was still half asleep, I nodded.

He approached and knelt down next to where I sat, hand on the arm of the chair as he studied me carefully and calculated his next move. I tried to focus myself and make sense of everything that was unravelling, but my body was still weak and sluggish from whatever I had been laced with. I sat silently, waiting for him to make his move.

"Mairi, I know you're confused. I know you want answers; I think we need to talk." He so spoke softly that one could almost believe the sincerity of his tone, if they didn't know the truth. He stood, looking slightly unsure and twiddling his fingers as he continued, "There's so much to tell you Mairi, but I'm not quite sure where to star—"

As he spoke the door came crashing open, the familiar form of Morgan appearing in the doorway as she stepped over two fresh corpses. I couldn't see Bram as I anxiously looked for him. Morgan stepped forward, looking straight at the Professor she smirked and said, "Hello, Alistair."

I had a feeling I was still missing a piece of the puzzle.

Arm raised she revealed a gun, solely focused on the Professor. She slowly approached, putting distance between me and him. As she came level with me she spoke, not taking her eyes off her target, "Mairi are you ok? Are you hurt?"

My brain still not cooperating I managed to speak in a mumble, "Fine, just sluggish, soup was off I think."

Satisfied I was as ok as could be, she proceeded to focus her attention on the Professor with a fire in her eyes I didn't know could exist; such intense passion and hatred. "You know why I'm here Alistair, where is she? I want her back. I will end you if you don't give her to me."

He didn't react and he wasn't surprised by her questions. But his eyes did momentarily flick in my direction for a split second, was he worried about me? Or was he hoping I'd intervene and try to save him? Stuttering and stammering he eventually began to speak.

"Morgan, there's a child in the room. You wouldn't hurt me in front of a young girl, would you? That's not you, you're a scientist, not a killer."

She smirked.

"You'd better check with Miles about that," said Morgan with a smile on her face that did not reach her cold eyes. "Oh wait, that might be a bit difficult. Last chance. I want answers."

The Professor looked mildly shocked about Miles but didn't comment, instead he carried on, "Look, we can work this out Morgan. I still love you and I know you still love me, we can be a family again, just the three of us." He was nervously shuffling about trying, to calm her down. I could see him desperately trying to formulate his next move. My body still sluggish, I tried to muster my energy to be ready to move.

"A FAMILY!" Morgan screamed as she raised the gun to point directly at his head, her hand shaking in anger. "You took my family from me! You stole her from me and even now you're trying to hide her!"

Morgan was becoming angrier by the moment, the cool-headed woman I first met was extinct; replaced by a red-headed warrior of vengeance and fire, ready to attack. He backed himself against his table, unable to go any further he continued speaking while trying to look for an escape route.

"I'm not hiding anything she's right there! Can't you see? Can't you even recognize your own daughter?" His arm pointed straight at me and I froze in shock. He must be lying, he had to be trying to distract her and it was working; her arm faltered slightly as she dropped her gaze from him.

She glanced at me again, one word escaping her lips, "Isla?" Her biggest mistake.

All that twitching and shuffling he'd been doing had been nothing more than a distraction. As if in slow motion, I watched as he pulled a weapon from under his desk. She didn't even notice, still looking at me dazed and mumbling as if only seeing me for the very first time.

"Isla? My darling Isla, all along it's been you."

But I noticed, and so did my warrior. As he trained the gun towards her, Morgan, my *mother*. She finally broke out from whatever prison had been keeping her from me. The switch was instant and I wasn't stupid enough to resist. I heard the click of the shot, the whistle as the bullet left the gun. I moved effortlessly. Face to face with my mother finally, lovingly looking at me as I stood in front of her but completely unaware of the danger I was hiding as she finally found the answers she had been searching for all these years.

The whole world slowed as the bullet pierced through my skin, digging through my back, treacherously burying itself further in; the adrenaline in my system holding me up as I kept my gaze locked on my mother, the woman who had been in front of me all along. Her face slowly dropped with realization as my body finally betrayed me and slumped. She caught me in her arms, shock setting in she started screaming at me and rocking me in her arms.

"No, please don't leave me Isla! I've searched too long to lose you now, how did I not see you right in front of me, please don't leave me," she cried out, lowering herself to the floor as she cradled me in her arms. The world blurred but I could vaguely make out my father's figure slowly disappearing. My body must have been in complete shock as I slowly slipped into darkness. I had finally found my answers, no need to run anymore; I could finally rest. But I wasn't ready to leave, I finally had something to live for, she had been in front of me all this time. My mother's tear-stained face slipped away as I tried to desperately hold on to her image in my mind while the coldness set in.

Twenty-Seven: Bram

Bram waited outside the room, uneasily waiting for Morgan's orders. He had reluctantly let her go in alone but he didn't have to feel comfortable about it. Part of him had wanted to follow her, but he knew better; never disobey orders. He had been trying to listen from outside, but even with his keen sense of hearing and his ear pressed up against the door he could not hear so much as a murmur from inside. This did not reassure him in the slightest.

He turned to the team that was still with him and proceeded to split them up into smaller groups, spreading them in both directions in case another attack came their way. Never leave anything to chance, fail to plan and you plan to fail. Failure was never an option.

He sent two out as scouts to recon the building and report back on the situation. As they disappeared out of sight, his radio crackled. "Precious packages located and secured, however we are still encountering unfriendly parties and require extra support to secure safe extraction of the packages."

Bram thought, debating what to do. Morgan had said the extraction was the priority; the mission priority had to come first. At the back of his mind he was thinking, Mairi could be there, needing help. But he couldn't leave Morgan either. He radioed back, "Support on route, hold your position."

He nodded to his two teams guarding the perimeter and sent them on their way. Only him left now until the scouts returned; if they returned. But he couldn't jeopardise the mission and he wasn't leaving Morgan. He positioned himself as best as he could; back against the door, checking all points routinely.

Bram had never questioned Morgan, he had never disobeyed her orders and he was loyal to a fault. He didn't know any other way to be. However, he had never been worried about her before today.

As he watched her take the life of another, possibly the first life she had ever taken, he noticed the change. It happened to them all in one way or another, but you were never the same after taking the life of another human being, no matter how much they deserved it, and it worried him how the change would affect her. Everyone coped differently, some better than others. That's what decided whether you were cut out for this job. The first was always the one you remembered most clearly. He could still taste the vomit in his mouth from where he had puked afterwards. It was swift and clean, there was no begging or pleading. It had been a simple choice; kill or be killed. But in those moments afterwards Bram could still remember staring into those soulless eyes as they laid wide open, judging him, condemning him, sentencing him for his actions. Everyone's first was different, but nobody was ever the same afterwards.

Trying to stay focused on the task at hand, his mind drifted to Mairi, a puzzle in her own right. A perfect assassin, who could kill more effectively than most soldiers, and a fragile young girl who battled with the horrors of what she had done to survive. Two completely mismatched people sharing one body, trying to fit together as best they could.

That moment when she had returned for him at the roadside, she had appeared like his guardian angel – protecting him, saving him – and he had never been more grateful. For the first time since that first life he took, he had thought he was going to die. Although he wasn't afraid of death, relief had flooded over him as she leapt into action to keep him in the land of living for at least a little bit longer.

Bram's radio crackled drawing his attention.

"Extraction in progress packages on the move."

He breathed a short sigh of relief, at least something was going to plan, but they weren't out of the woods yet. He leant into his radio to reply, "Proceed with extraction, eliminate threats with any force necessary, do you understand?"

"Understood."

Bram heard a noise coming; gun poised, he readied himself. As he watched a figure appear around the corner, he realised it was one of his scouts. He was dragging something – the other scout. Bram rushed over to try and help but it was already too late. The trail of blood that showed the path they had taken had been too great and the scout spluttered slightly before succumbing to his injuries.

Bram respectfully touched his face, slowly closing the fallen soldier's eyes for the last time. He looked like he was peacefully slumbering. It was never easy losing anyone but it was a common occurrence in their line of work. He remembered every face, every name, remembering it could have easily been him each time. He desperately wanted to barge into the room, the waiting was killing him; he needed to know if Morgan was ok. There was only one door in and out, no alternative escapes. He only hoped she had found the answers she was looking for in there.

As he paced anxiously trying to keep his composure, his companion swept the corridors looking for any signs of threats but more so keeping himself busy so as to not think of their comrade still lying on the floor nearby.

The world stopped. An all too familiar sound, from a place that made his heart sink. His companion glanced at him as Bram spoke, "Stay here." It wasn't a request.

Crashing into the room, expecting the worst, he found a scene beyond his deepest fears.

He found Morgan knelt on the floor with her back to him. She didn't even acknowledge him, instead she carried on hysterically screaming and crying her words as they completely melted into one and he couldn't work out what she was saying.

"Morgan, what's going on? What's happened?" Then he saw. She was holding something in her arms. No not something, someone.

"No, No, No…" He didn't even notice the words leave his mouth. Morgan's hands were covered in blood as she still cradled Mairi's lifeless body. What had happened? How could this have happened? Bram listened numbly as Morgan continued talking to the figure in her arms.

"No, Isla my sweet Isla, please don't leave me… I've only just found you, please come back," she sobbed uncontrollably. Bram lowered himself down while his brain tried to work out what was going on.

"Sssshhhh Morgan, that's not your Isla; we haven't found her yet, that's Mairi. That's not your daughter."

Morgan's head snapped up bleary-eyed, "Don't you get it? Don't you understand? She IS my daughter! All this time right there in front of us, and I let her lead us straight back here to her death. She died protecting me! It's all my fault."

She melted into hysterics and would not loosen her grip on the body.

Bram wasn't sure if any of this was true but he knew either way his heart was racing and his stomach was spinning, threatening to bring up any remaining breakfast he may have had.

He looked dazed at Mairi's peaceful-looking face, blood smeared on her cheeks from Morgan's hands. How could this have happened? He had been outside the whole time, who could have done this?

"Morgan, I need you to listen to my voice," he said trying to calm her enough to reach her, "I need you to tell me who did this, I need to know what happened. Who did this to Mairi?"

Morgan's eyes lifted slowly from the child she cradled so desperately and her words spat with venom, "Alistair Crowland. Her father. He murdered her, while trying to murder me." The conviction in her voice started to waver and her voice cracked., "She saw what he was going to do… and she saved me. She died looking into my eyes… she died, held in my arms. How could I let this happen?" Her body slumped, drained.

Still in shock and trying to process everything, Bram kicked himself into action. He couldn't think about Mairi for the moment, he needed to focus, for both her and Morgan.

"Morgan, look at me. Focus. You are in shock, but the time for grieving must wait. We need to find Alistair, we need to find him and make him pay for what he's done." That got her attention.

"But I can't leave her alone, she can't be left. I've only just found her,"

Morgan pleaded. Bram looked around before signalling to his companion who was still covering the door, "You stay here, guard her and do not let anyone touch or move her until we return."

He nodded.

Bram turned to Morgan, gently releasing her grip on Mairi and saying, "Morgan, we need to go. I don't know what he looks like. I need you with me, she will be safe here and we will come straight back for her I promise. Look, I've got a guard to watch over her, I promise we won't leave her again."

Morgan reluctantly placed the lifeless body down on the floor. Kissing her gently on the forehead, she whispered, "I'll be back soon Isla; I promise I'll be back."

Bram realised Morgan was traumatised, but he knew every second wasted was distance that Mairi's killer was using to get away from them. Reloading his weapon, he gave Morgan a hand up from the floor and began to survey the room for Alistair's exit.

He immediately noticed a bookcase that looked out of place and as he approached he realised it was a door, opening it up it revealed a corridor. They needed to make up speed if they had any chance of catching up with him.

With one last glance at the body currently being guarded as he felt that sickening twist in his stomach, he pushed it down and focused on the here and now.

Twenty-Eight: Alistair

Morgan sat cradling her daughter in her arms, begging and pleading as she rocked the small figure, desperately trying to keep her awake as her world was once more ripped from her. As those beautiful eyes closed, not a breath was felt again from the lifeless body gripped tightly in her embrace.

Alistair knew time was running out, part of him had wanted to try and reach out and console her but he knew that time had passed. He had murdered her daughter, their daughter. There was no going back now, he had to escape before reinforcements arrived. Grabbing the USB from the laptop and making his departure as the room filled, a whispered apology escaping his lips.

He knew that the board would need to know of these events immediately.

The world crashed in around Morgan as Bram stormed into the room, brought in by the alert of the gunshot. She was completely oblivious to him, feeling the last fragments of her heart shatter. Her only lifeline, her reason for living all this time had been destroyed before her eyes. She held her daughter in her arms but knew she couldn't do anything to stop it.

And the demon who had caused it was gone as soon as the unforgivable deed had been done, vanished in the commotion of destruction he had brought.

She slumped, still holding the body, refusing to let go; if she didn't let go then it wasn't real.

Alistair fumbled around clumsily, grabbing a phone from his pocket while trying to keep up a speedy pace. Dialling the number, he waited. It rang twice before connecting and he spoke as calmly as he could manage in his out-of-breath state, still moving through the dusty corridors.

"Institute compromised, missing product in my office, out of action. Heading to extraction point, initiate emergency protocols and notify the board." Alistair hung up. There was no point waiting for a reply, they were most likely already aware. He still didn't know how Morgan and her team had managed to find the Institute, it would take months to rebuild elsewhere and then restock. His head hurt just thinking about it, the board would not be happy.

As his mind momentarily replayed the events that had taken place, one thought kept replaying; the child, his child… gone. In the eyes of the board she was merely a product just like all the others but he'd managed to protect her all these years, keeping her off the client lists and safe at the Institute. He knew it wouldn't have worked forever but he had done the best he could. In the end though, he realised he couldn't save her from the one danger he hadn't foreseen, himself.

The phone rang, pulling him from his self-pity. He answered and listened as a male voice relayed, "Protocols already underway, product recovery in progress. Extraction point ready, ensure you have the files and are ready for debrief." The line went dead. No room for questions or negotiation. He checked his pocket to ensure the USB drive was intact. Alistair knew it was the only protection he had; all of the information needed to ensure he was still valuable enough to the board for them to extract him and keep him alive, for now at least.

As he began to ascend the steep stairs, his legs ached. The steps were so dusty they looked like they hadn't been used in years. Reaching the top of the staircase he pushed against the door, it wouldn't move. Panic set in. He pushed harder and the door shifted slightly, then with a final deep push it swung open revealing the rooftop. He just hoped the evacuation team arrived in time.

Stepping out onto the rooftop, his eyes tried adjusting to the light. A light breeze swept across his face, the refreshing cool air a welcoming relief to the dusty corridors. As Alistair surveyed the surroundings, he could see small dots running around in various locations on the ground. He couldn't tell who they belonged to, so he stepped back slightly to keep well out of view.

He turned with horror towards the door he had come through, realising it was still open. Pushing it with all his weight he managed to close it, hoping it would slow anyone trying to follow behind. As he dusted himself off he could hear the familiar sound of a helicopter approaching. In the distance, over the forest behind the Institute, he could see the black aircraft approaching. As it headed right for him, part of him was trembling and slightly worried in case it wasn't the ride he was expecting.

As it got closer the wind picked up, causing his eyes to squint. He crouched slightly, ensuring his feet were firmly grounded. As it lowered itself noisily towards the small rooftop a figure stuck his head out, beckoning him over.

He knew he didn't have a choice; it was either go or return and face Morgan, who he knew wouldn't exactly be waiting to welcome him with open arms. Alistair braced his body as the downward force from the rotor blades sent the winds gushing towards him. Keeping as low as possible he waited for the approaching aircraft to extract him, his heart hammering as time slowed.

An extended hand reached out to help him in. He breathed a sigh of relief as he entered the helicopter; he was safe at least for now.

"Hello Professor, we are your extraction team, how many for extraction?"

He could barely hear over the noise but managed to reply, "Just one for extraction, we need to move quickly though."

Nodding, the man signalled to the pilot before strapping Alistair in and bracing for take-off. As he felt the helicopter begin to lift, he could see movement from the dusty doorway. His heart pounded, willing the pilot to move faster.

As the door swung open, two figures appeared. A young male, followed by a blood-stained Morgan. He just about heard her scream his name as they pulled away, a pang in his chest causing an uncomfortable feeling as he looked at her remorsefully; the words, 'I'm sorry' escaping his lips.

He knew he would have to pay one day, for all he had done. And every day until then he would have to live with the regrets, every single one.

Twenty-Nine: Morgan

The exit Bram had found was an old dusty passage full of turns and uneven floors, both he and Morgan moved as fast as they could through the constricted space. Bram kept glancing back at Morgan, checking she was still behind him; she was a ticking time bomb now and he needed to keep a close eye on her.

"Don't keep wasting time looking back at me Bram, keep moving; we need to make up ground." She wasn't about to be stopped or deterred, nothing else mattered now. She had lost everything, she would make sure Alistair did too if it was the last thing she did. She had nothing left to lose and that made her even more dangerous.

They came to a staircase, no other routes available than up. Bram cautiously took the lead, not trusting Morgan's judgement now as he had a feeling she was on a one-way mission with no plan for a return journey. As they climbed the stairs they could hear a noise, loud and deafening, coming from the roof. They both picked up speed, not wanting to lose their target.

As they got to the top, the door was closed. Bram rammed it with all the strength he could muster, barely moving the door. He went at it again and again, desperately trying to break it down until, with a final shove, the door gave way as the pair of them realized they were too late.

The helicopter, hovered over the roof as Alistair desperately clambered in.

Morgan screamed at the top of her lungs, "ALISTAIR!"

His head sprung round, clearly alarmed to see the pair of them heading towards him as he ushered the pilot to move quicker. Eyes locked with Morgan he mouthed 'I'm sorry' as his transport began to lift him higher.

Morgan, lost as to what to do next, slumped on the floor broken and distraught. She had failed again. Bram however knew it wasn't over yet. As the helicopter began to gain height, he knew exactly what to do. Out of one of his many pockets, he pulled a small item no bigger than his hand. Using his teeth, he pulled a pin out of the top and glanced down at the grenade so delicately sat in his hands, it had been a while since he'd needed to use one of these.

Taking a deep breath, his eyes never tore away from the helicopter. He took a run up towards the edge and lobbed the grenade towards it. He held his breath as he saw it roll onto the floor of the helicopter through the still-open door Alistair had clambered into. Everything moved in slow motion, but the impact was almost instant and the explosion that followed soon grabbed Morgan's attention as she watched with grim satisfaction as the helicopter plummeted in a blazing ball of fire towards the dense forest below, resulting in a dramatic explosion on impact. There was no way he was surviving that.

The mission had been completed, the Professor had been removed from duty... permanently and the Institute would be no more. The pair wearily dragged themselves down the stairs and back towards the harsh realities they still needed to face.

Morgan was silent and sombre as she led the path back to the room where her world had ended before her eyes, Bram following closely behind and still not sure how to process the day's events. However, when they returned they quickly realised something wasn't right.

Where Mairi's body had been delicately laid to rest there was a blood-stained carpet and a missing body, yet even more horrifying was the dead guard found by the doorway. Clean shot to the head, he hadn't stood a chance. Bram began kicking himself, another life lost, when was the price just too high?

Morgan stood silent, staring at the spot where she had left her daughter's body, guarded and protected. Her world crumbling even further into darkness and despair.

"Why would someone take her from me again? Not even in death can they leave her alone. We need to find her Bram; we can't abandon her again."

Bram radioed all the teams, pulling them all into the mass search for Mairi's missing body. Every room, cupboard and secret area was turned. Walls were destroyed and piece by piece they took the building apart. But Mairi's body couldn't be found anywhere, neither could the files with all the details of the Institute; every computer had been wiped and all traces were gone as far as they could find. Morgan wasn't giving up though and even when ordered to return to base had refused until Bram had persuaded her that the answers they needed would not be found there.

"Morgan, we need to go, she wouldn't want us here chasing our tails, she'd want us out there hunting down the rest of them." Bram had begun to resign himself to the fact that they might never discover what happened to Mairi's body, but he knew he had to keep Morgan distracted to allow her to process her grief. His heart broke every time he thought of her, his guardian angel, fallen but not forgotten.

"You're right, we're going to find them," she paused staring into space, "We're going to find every last one of them and we are going to make them pay."

Thirty: Epilogue

The clink of the footsteps against the cold floor echoed throughout the corridor. As she approached the double doors, she leaned in causing the doors to part. As they swung heavily behind her, a figure appeared standing with his back to her, his white lab coat smeared with red.

"Any trouble extracting the package?" she demanded.

"Just one minor delay but it was resolved swiftly, everything's here." The doctor turned to her, adjusting his rimmed glasses that had slipped down his nose.

She approached the metal trolley with its covered contents and a small cold hand slipped from the flat metal surface, dangling down, exposed. She gently placed it back under the white sheet before exiting the room and heading down the corridor to her next point of business, the doctor shuffling closely behind. She approached a room with a small window and glanced in briefly before turning the handle and entering through the single door.

"What do we know?" she asked quietly.

The doctor nervously began looking through his charts before replying, "He was the only one to be extracted along with the package, no other survivors unfortunately."

Irrelevant, she thought, it just meant another clean-up crew needed to remove any traces of the incident.

"And what's the update on him?" She did not like to be kept waiting and could not stand idle chatter. Why say something in a hundred words that you could say in five? Inefficient and counterproductive. Luckily, the doctor knew the harsh whip of her tongue enough not to dawdle.

"Well, ma'am. He was barely alive when we got him and will require extensive surgery and possible reconstruction in places. He is in an induced coma now until we can begin work, we were just waiting to find out if you wanted us to commence work or terminate?"

Tempting, oh so tempting after the screw-ups he had caused, but unfortunately he was needed. With Miles gone too, they were too thin on the ground. He could always be retired later if he outlived his purpose. She turned to the doctor dramatically, "No, of course not! Professor Crowland is a respected and important member of our team and it is imperative that we do everything we can to save him, do whatever you need to."

The doctor didn't look convinced by her words but he wasn't dumb enough to open his mouth.

She left the ward again, satisfied that the programme was still salvageable. From the first reports back the GAP taskforce were still blissfully unaware of the Shadow Board's involvement, but this was one close call too many. Measures would need to be taken to ensure this didn't happen again.

Time to report back to the board and then begin relocating and rebuilding the Institute, clients couldn't be kept waiting after all.

Also from Tiny Tree Books

Printed in Great Britain
by Amazon